All Hollow

ALSO BY SIMEON COURTIE

The Long and Whining Road

"A great read!" Lynne Truss, BBC Radio 4

London Book Festival Grand Prize Winner 2012
USA Book News winner 2013
Readers' Favourite Gold Award 2013
Shirley You Jest winner 2013
IPPY Award, 'Travel' winner 2013

All Hollow

A Dark Horror. Literally.

SIMEON COURTIE

with Hal Stewart

First published in Great Britain by Simantics Ltd

Copyright © Simeon Courtie 2019

Printed and bound by Gomer Press Ltd., Ceredigion, Wales

Cover design by ebooklaunch.com

This is a work of fiction. All characters, organisations and events are either products of the author's imagination or are used fictitiously.

First Edition

A catalogue record for this book is available from the British Library.

ISBN 978 0 9571980 2 9

eISBN 978 0 9571980 3 6

Preface

I had the idea for setting a horror inside the tunnels of Gibraltar after a generous army officer with a huge set of keys gave me a private tour in 2011. I was working on the Rock for a short time as a presenter on the forces radio station BFBS. A few years later when my producer friend, Hal, and I decided to write a horror screenplay, those tunnels called from the dark.

As ardent fans of the genre we wanted to take some standard horror tropes and twist them in an unexpected way, pull the rug out from beneath the feet of fans like us. Later, when I decided to write the story as the book you hold now, we discussed changes. One was whether those caricatures were too derivative, obsolete even, in 2019. Ultimately, horror won. Fans will enjoy spotting recognisable character-types, each a little altered, each luring the reader into a false sense of the familiar. For those new to the genre, welcome! It's four friends going on holiday. What can possibly go wrong?

All Hollow

One

Sunshine, money, pleasure, death; these are the trades of a rock called Gibraltar. A geographical anomaly, a crooked spit of land, an angry stone that God shook from his shoe, she dangles from Spain's southern shores, clings like a parasite, proudly independent of her host, and yet unable to let go. A fortified arsenal for over a thousand years, from 7th-century Moors to the modern British military, the Rock's importance as a strategic location between Europe and Africa, as a gateway from the North Atlantic to the Mediterranean Sea, waned in peace-time Europe. Her teeth lost their bite. By the early 21st-century she had fewer guns but more cash. Gibraltar's 'off-shore' British status made her a tax-efficient base for hundreds of banks. Duty-free alcohol and tobacco lured a regular supply of cruise liners, spilling their bloated contents onto cobbled streets to ravenously consume endless offers of bargain booze and cheap cigarettes.

Into this peculiar melting pot of isolated British locals, dispassionate military personnel and sun-blushed tourists flew a young woman who wasn't supposed to be there.

By the age of twenty-five Petra's life was supposed to have been sorted. The Masters would have led to a PhD then a research post, maybe an overseas project in South America or Madagascar. She'd be Dr Petra Collins, making waves, pushing boundaries, using her knowledge and passion for microbiology to discover new species, new bacteria, new antibiotics. She'd be saving the planet, saving the human race. But instead she was in a cramped seat on a cheap airline, barely able to save herself from the wreckage of a relationship she'd left behind.

'You all right, hun?' asked Carly, her recently rediscovered school friend in the seat next to her.

Petra squirmed, freeing her feet into the carpeted aisle. 'Sure.'

For the chance to stretch her legs occasionally on the short flight from London, she'd sacrificed the window seat and was now trying to glimpse a view across her neighbours' laps. Those laps belonged to Carly and her boyfriend, Dane, who'd bagged the window seat. Across the aisle to Petra's right was the fourth member of this last-minute holiday troupe, Krishna, Dane's mate from work. Krishna was glued to his phone.

As the plane banked for its final approach, the oval window presented a view of Gibraltar that you don't see in promotional videos. Rather than a sparkling sea lapping at the feet of a majestic jewel of the Mediterranean, Petra saw leaden clouds press down on angry, frothing waves that boiled and chomped at a giant, jagged rock pointing crookedly towards them. The mountainous grey wedge wore a shawl of speckled green down one side. On its peak flew a Union Jack, pulled taut in a bracing wind. As they descended, Petra picked out streets and buildings scattered around the edges. Then a sudden jolt of turbulence shook everyone to attention, filling the cabin with gasps and nervous laughter.

Carly's manicured, lilac-painted nails were digging into Dane's strong grip. 'He can cut that out for a start.' She frowned towards the front of the plane. Petra smiled, sank back into her seat, and let the aircraft be jostled and buffeted by the wind.

'Poniente,' Krishna said, holding his phone screen towards her.

'Sorry?'

'The Poniente. That's what this is.'

'The plane?'

'The wind. Look.' He jiggled his phone for her attention. 'New app, like Wiki for weather. Says that this morning Gibraltar will get the Poniente.' He read from the screen: 'a fresh westerly wind that blows in from the Atlantic.'

'Ah, OK then. Good knowledge. I thought using phones on planes was against the rules.'

'Hooked it up to the WiFi … on a plane! That blows my mind, and only cost me eight quid.'

'Right.' Petra nodded, pretending that was good value. The aircraft tipped and shimmied. Beyond Krishna were an American couple who squeezed each other's hand, and beyond them, the runway loomed large in the window.

'Want to look?' He offered the sleek, shiny handset to her again. Krishna's cheeks were podgy when he smiled, his stubble perfectly groomed within symmetrical lines, like a neat child's colouring-in.

'It's fine, thanks.'

The bang as the plane slammed into the concrete was accompanied by screams and chaos as several overhead lockers sprang open and bags became missiles. With a terrifying *SWISH* a broken-glass guillotine blade sliced through the air past Petra's face, missed her shoulder by millimetres and shattered on the floor closely followed by a crashing picture frame.

Above the shrill yelps of Carly deafening her left ear, Petra heard Krishna shout, 'Are you OK?' The smashed glass was scattered around a dark print of an oil painting in a broken ornate frame: Jesus surrounded by gesticulating bodies, pointing to a man wrapped in cloth.

The plane slowed to a dawdle as if clattering to the ground like a tossed toy was all in a day's work, and Petra breathed again. The relaxed drawl of the captain came over the speakers, a voice like honey, an accent like that of an old-money cad. "Good morning, ladies and gentlemen, welcome to Gibraltar.

5

Apologies if you felt a slight bump back there. Bit breezy for the old kite this morning. Almost spilled my Martini. Hu, hu, hrrrr."

'Is he joking?' Carly was cross. 'Is he havin' a bleedin' laugh? My mate nearly died back 'ere!' she shouted.

'Shhhh, it's fine.' Petra patted her hand.

'You could've lost a bloody arm!'

Dishevelled passengers were unpicking themselves from the debris of bags and jackets while the embarrassed American woman was leaning across Krishna's lap to apologise to Petra. The painting was Jesus raising Lazarus. She'd seen it at the National Gallery in London. They'd paid extra for the frame. The husband was shaking his head. He'd told her they could get it framed back home, but would she listen?

'Really,' Petra reassured everyone. 'I'm fine!'

SOME TIME AROUND the middle of the afternoon, the wind dropped, the sun appeared and there was only one obvious place for the friends to go. The Rock beckoned.

6

'Long way from Harlow, right?' smiled Carly.

'Hmmmm.' Petra was gazing across the glittering sea from their high vantage point on a steep path leading up the side of Gibraltar's central feature, over a thousand feet of towering grey limestone. They'd lost the boys a few turns back on the winding path up from the town, and she now took in the view, hands on hips. As she leaned into a large shrub to sniff at a clump of its orange flowers, Carly gestured to Petra's top and said, 'This is nice. Work?'

'Of course. Forty per cent discount.'

'It's lush, I love it.'

The top was nothing special, a fairly cheap T-shirt with a subtle white and silver-grey camouflage pattern. She wore slim denim shorts almost to the knee and faded red Converse pumps. Almost everything Petra wore was from the high street clothing shop where she worked. As an assistant manager, she wasn't obliged to be 'on brand' while working, but the hefty discount meant her wardrobe barely left that label, that season, from the rails in that actual shop. While they waited for the boys to catch them up she reached behind her head, effortlessly slid a hair-

7

band onto her wrist and released the clutch of braided Afro hair into a springy mop. With a shake of her head the braids whipped around, dropping into a curtain across her face. She grinned at Carly through twisted strands.

'Beautiful,' her friend agreed.

'I *am*, aren't I?' said Petra, standing strong and pushing her chest out. They both laughed and Petra pulled her hair back into a surprisingly neat, braided ponytail, snapping the hair-band into a double loop with expert speed.

Petra was taller and broader than her friend. Physically, they were complete opposites. Carly was petite and blonde. Her ample chest and pinched waist had made her a boy-magnet since she and Petra had become friends at secondary school. Petra had been stocky, muscular, a mixed-race athlete without the passion for athletics. From the age of thirteen Petra realised that most of the boys who showed an interest in her were in fact trying to get closer to Carly. That was fine. Petra wasn't as confident around boys as her mate, so she was happier keeping out of their way. It wasn't until they parted after Sixth Form that Petra discovered the opposite sex. Maybe she'd needed to be out of Carly's shadow. Carly could never be outshone.

'Seriously, Petra, thanks for coming. I couldn't believe it when you said yes.'

'Don't be silly. If you hadn't found me on Facebook God knows what I'd be doing now. Languishing – no, *festering* – at home. Except it's not home. It's a room. A room in a shared house. I'd be festering "at room".'

Carly's face creased with concern. 'It won't be for long, hun.'

'Seriously. Thanks for the lifeline. We lose touch for almost six years and you find me at the exact moment I need a friend. Textbook Carly.'

'How is everything … with Zach?'

'Oh, no change. Definitely over. I haven't heard from him since that drunk text I told you about. I think he's got the message.'

'You definitely don't want him back, then?'

'No way. Definitely not.'

'Was he that bad? I wish I'd met him.'

Petra thought about this for a moment. 'To be fair he wasn't awful. But if you'd seen the texts he sent that girl. More than just workmates, if you get my drift.'

'Dick.'

'We were falling out a bit even before that, to be honest.'

'I still can't believe you've deleted all your pictures. What did he look like?'

'Who can I compare him to? Y'know Professor Brian Cox?'

'The hot scientist off the TV? If Zach looks like him *I* want his number!'

'No, he doesn't, but I kind of thought he did. I was bedazzled by his PhD and his … geekiness, I suppose.'

'Geekiness? Oh Jesus, Petra found herself a nerd. I coulda told you that would happen back at school.'

'I *am* a nerd, or had you forgotten, Little Miss Cheerleader?'

'Fair enough,' smiled her old comrade.

'It was the gaming in the end. I probably could've forgiven the inappropriate texts, but we were already doomed. There were three of us in the relationship: me, Zach and whatever game he was currently addicted to. There's a limit to how excited I can get about conquering another planet in Hyperiums.'

'Sorry, what?'

'Java-coded text-based multiplayer.'

'Cheers. Much clearer.'

'I mean, I miss him, of course I do, but I think

what I actually miss is the apartment, the regular rhythm of our routines, cooking for two, all that.'

'Bloody hell, Petra, you sound like an old woman! He isn't dead! And neither are you! We're twenty-five! In our prime, girl!'

'Correct, Miss Porter! Which is why I leapt at your invite to ...' She looked around. '... possibly the weirdest holiday destination I've ever seen.'

Carly rolled her eyes. 'Dane's idea. S'OK, though. We'll have a laugh, won't we?'

'He seems lovely. All outdoorsy and ... fit! You're a lucky girl, Carls.'

'Yeah, he'll do. For now.' She cackled and they saw two men round the corner on the path below them. 'Here they come.'

'Let's see the ring again.'

Carly splayed the back of her hand towards her friend. A glittering rock shone from her third finger.

Petra examined it closely. 'I love it. Every time I look at it I love it more. It looked good in the airport, but now we're in the sun ... wow. What stone is that?'

'The lavender colour is tanzanite. In Chinese culture it means long life and good fortune.'

'And you love a Chinese.'

Carly laughed. 'The middle's diamond, obvs. I wasn't gonna let him get away with anything less.'

'Carly gets her way. How unusual.' Petra raised an eyebrow. 'I hope Dane knows what he's in for.' She returned her attention to the flowering shrubs, running her fingers through them to release the heavy scent, and then pushing her head into them like a botanist, inhaling their perfume.

The two men approached and Carly called out, 'Take your time!' The taller man, Dane, wore khaki cargo pants, clean trainers and a tight blue T-shirt that did nothing to hide his muscular torso. He had the short-cropped hair and lazy smile of a catalogue model, not the sales executive he was. On first meeting him just hours before, Petra's initial thought had been, 'classic Carly'. She watched Krishna puffing alongside him, rounder in shape, baggier of clothing, and looking altogether less athletic. More like asthmatic. His roomy shorts and Hawaiian shirt were a bold look. Petra smiled at them and heard Krishna saying to Dane, 'It's the *little* monkeys that freak me out. Perched in dark corners like tiny evil old men.'

Dane ignored him and smiled at Carly, slipping a hand around her waist.

She said, 'What took you? *You're* supposed to be the climber.'

'Krishna and that bloody phone. Had to spend ten minutes setting up his carbon fibre selfie-stick.'

'*You* didn't have to sit next to him on the plane,' Petra chipped in.

'Most expensive phone on the market and no idea how to use it,' Dane added.

'Must've taken a dozen pictures of his feet.'

'Or his crotch.'

'Er …' interrupted Krishna, affronted. 'I'm right here, y'know.'

'How long are we going to be inside this rock?' Carly said. 'I am *not* going home without a tan.'

Krishna rummaged in the pockets of his baggy beige shorts, pulling out receipts, sweet wrappers and eventually a crumpled flyer. 'Says here … erm, about an hour.' Petra smirked and didn't believe for a moment that he'd read that anywhere.

'I came here for sun, sangria and sssssomething else,' winked Carly, pinching Dane's bum.

'Sangria?' said Dane. 'That's Spain, darlin'. Half an hour *that* way. This is Gibraltar. British through and through.'

'G and Ts all round,' smiled Krishna.

'Yeah, whatever. I can still get a tan *if* I'm not being dragged around some old cave.'

'It's not a cave, actually, Carly.' Krishna lectured. 'It's *tunnels*.'

'Great,' said Carly, her flat, bored voice hitting Krishna's withering tone right back at him.

'C'mon,' said Dane. 'Might be fun.'

'It'll be brilliant!' said Krishna, recharged and enthused. 'Miles of man-made tunnels, a whole town, hidden, sealed off for decades. They started doing tours last year. I watched a video on YouTube.'

'What's it like?' asked Carly.

'Dunno, it was completely black. Couldn't see a thing.'

'Really?'

He smirked. 'No, Carly. I'm joking. There are lights in there, tour guides, there's probably a gift shop. You're up for it, right, Petr – WOAH!' He recoiled and sprang away from her. Carly's head jerked around to the source of Krishna's shock and she squealed. A spider the size of a child's hand was on Petra's shoulder. Dane said, 'Holy shhh –' and was interrupted by Krishna.

'Stay. Very. Still.'

'What? What is it?' asked Petra, cocking her

head, trying to pull focus on whatever was behind her ear.

'Don't move!' squealed Carly.

Krishna swiped his thumb across his phone screen. 'Somewhere on here I've got an app for the coastguard.' Then they leaned back and made an 'OHHH' sound as the dark brown spider trod forwards across the brow of Petra's collar bone. Its earthy-coloured abdomen was bulbous and bore a dark brown stripe down its length. Each thick leg tapered to a hard, skeletal point. At the front of the spider's body were two clearly visible fangs curled under its head like holstered weapons.

Petra saw the distinctive shape and pulled her head back with a muffled yelp. Her heart pounded, but she didn't scream. She clamped her mouth shut and concentrated. Reaching across her chest, she placed the back of her hand to her shoulder as a flat platform and held it as still as adrenaline would allow. The spider, taking its cue, crept slowly forwards, placing its two front legs on her hand. The audience held their breath. After a cautious pause, the bony arachnid progressed forwards again. Krishna had his hand over his mouth. The moment the last leg lifted from Petra's shoulder, she started to move. In one gentle, balletic motion, she unwound herself and crouched, her spider-platform-hand gliding without shocks or jerks down to ground level.

'There you go,' she said with the affection most people have for a puppy or a baby bird. 'No hitchhiking today.'

As each long, agile leg, the colour of old bone, explored a way off Petra's hand onto the dirt of the path, Carly made a little retching sound. When Petra's passenger had disembarked, she stayed crouching, felt her breathing relax, and watched the huge thing tread with meticulous resolve over rocks and sticks and into the gloom of a shrub.

'Jesus, look at the size of that thing,' Dane said.

'Beautiful, in its way,' Petra murmured. 'I feel blessed.'

'Blessed?' Krishna baulked. 'I can't believe you didn't … I dunno, kill it. Swipe it off. Stamp on it.'

'Awwww, never,' Petra said, her nose crumpling at the thought.

'What, Petra?' said Carly. 'The world's greatest animal lover? I don't think so.'

'What species do you think that was?' Petra mused.

'Krishna's probably got an app for that,' joked Dane.

'Wolf spider, maybe?' she said as it crawled into

16

the undergrowth. 'They're common in Spain, so probably here, too.'

'At college Petra must've joined a million animal charities,' said Carly.

'Four,' Petra corrected.

'She nursed a hedgehog back to health when we were kids. Kept it in a shoebox. Called it Reebok. She wouldn't hurt a fly.'

'Unlike that thing,' added Dane, still watching the shrub cautiously.

'A fly?' said Krishna. 'That thing would eat a toddler. C'mon, let's go.'

As they walked up the path, Carly patted her friend and said, 'Gold star, Petra. Another life saved.'

Two

The sun was warm and welcome as they climbed the gentle gravel slope, each of them glowing and glistening. Krishna led the way, panting but purposeful.

Behind him, Petra said, 'Carly tells me you're a climber, Dane.'

'Boulderer, actually.' He smiled.

'That's not even a word,' piped Krishna.

'It's a sport,' his mate asserted.

'I'm Googling it.' Krishna pulled his large new phone from his pocket, where it had rested untroubled for almost half a minute.

'I've never been bouldering,' Petra said. 'But I did a bit of abseiling on a wildlife expedition in

Belize. Tight harness digging into your crotch and all that.'

'Ay, ay,' winked Carly. 'Fifty shades of Petra.'

This made Dane chuckle, then Krishna muttered at his phone screen, 'I think I've turned my central heating on.'

The effort of the climb was equal to Petra's effort to socialise with these new friends. A natural introvert, it would never have been her preference to spend a long weekend away with two strangers and a friend she hadn't seen for the last six years. The slump of post-break-up depression and a grinding resolve to pull herself out of her fug had prompted her to take a risk, grab at the opportunity dangled by long-lost Carly. She knew she'd find it hard, but she also knew she needed a jolt, new people, a change of scene.

Ignoring the twinge of jealousy she felt at the easy, tactile affection Dane showed Carly, she dug in. Made an effort. 'So, Krishna. If Dane's the climber ... sorry, boulderer. What about you?'

'He's the boulder,' Dane quipped.

Carly snorted a laugh but Krishna said, 'Ignore him, Petra. *We* do. Unfortunately I work with him, so that's my cross to bear.'

'What d'you do?'

19

'Sums, mainly. Data analyst is what my business card says.'

'When did they give you business cards?' asked Dane.

'All right – *would* say.'

Carly nudged Petra and said, 'Krishna's our nerdy friend, so I thought you'd get on.'

Petra clammed up, feeling the weight of the loaded statement, and was relieved when the corner of the path led around to a distraction: three people idly chatting at the entrance to a large, gloomy tunnel in the side of the Rock. One of them, an ageing Hispanic man in a light blue short-sleeved shirt, was sitting on a tatty camping chair at a small card table, typing on a heavy old laptop. Standing with him were a man and woman, both a little older than Petra, early thirties. He had an outdoor-man tan beneath his stubble, short-cropped hair, wore combat trousers, an army-green T-shirt and sturdy boots. The woman was toned, the strength that was visible in her arms and across her shoulders at odds with the softness of her face, a gentle oval with kind eyes framed by slightly shabby surfer-blonde curls. She wore a small backpack over her tight, short-sleeved checked shirt, cut-off combat trousers and open-toe beachcomber sandals.

'A-ha, just in time for the last tour of the day,' said the man, greeting the arrivals. 'Our online bookers, I assume.'

'Puram? Party of four?' asked the woman, picking up a clipboard from the tiny table.

'That's us, I'm Krishna.'

'Welcome,' smiled the man, shaking Krishna's hand. 'I'm Ed, this is Mary, and this cheerful chap is Hector. Say hello, Hector.'

The Spanish man's cracked-leather face maintained the crumpled frown of a disgruntled bulldog. He said nothing.

'I hope you remembered your passports,' said Mary, with a warm smile. 'If you could give those to Hector, please.' The gang fished out their passports from bags and pockets while she went on. 'You can trust Hector with them. He's a professional.'

'He actually is,' confirmed Ed. 'When he's not working for us he's a border guard down there.' He pointed down to the distant crossing between Gibraltar and Spain.

'How easy is it to get into Spain?' asked Petra. 'We're here for a few days.'

Ed took her passport and flicked it open, looking for her name. 'I'm glad you asked that … Petra Collins. First amazing fact of the tour,' he announced to the group. 'Gibraltar is not an island. It's an isthmus.'

'And a merry isthmus to you too,' said Krishna.

Petra smirked but Carly rolled her eyes. 'Sorry about him,' she said to Ed. 'My boyfriend brought him.'

Dane cocked his head and corrected her. 'Fiancé.'

'Oh God, yeh!' she squealed. 'I forgot! Oops.'

'Congratulations,' smiled Mary.

'Thanks, hun,' whispered Carly as Ed continued.

'An isthmus basically means it's joined on, not an island; so should the delights of Gibraltar not be enough, beyond that border crossing is Spain, Africa, the world.'

'Believe me,' said Mary, 'there have been many Gibraltarians who've taken that short walk and never come back.'

'To give you an idea of how easy it is, we often go over there just for dinner. Our favourite tapas bar is only half an hour walk from here in La Línea.' He pointed somewhere towards the coast across the water. 'You should check it out one evening. I'll give you the details. '

'Krishna, I've got your mobile number,' Mary said. 'I'll send you a link. The food is delicious.'

'If you're lucky you might even see Hector on your way through.' The sour-faced Spaniard glowered at his screen. 'We always give him a smile and a wave even if he's not in the passport booth,' Ed continued. 'He controls all the cameras!'

Krishna was standing at the small table, the last to hand over his passport. Hector had placed each passport on a small scanner that had beeped and sent all of their details to his screen. He was holding out his hand for the final one but Krishna seemed reluctant to give it to a surly stranger with unkempt grey hair and a sweat-stained shirt . 'Why do you need my passport?' Krishna asked.

Hector took the dark red booklet, shrugged a little, looked him straight in the eyes and said in a deadpan tone, 'I scan it so I can sell your bio-data.'

Dane laughed but Krishna and Hector looked deadly serious.

Ed stepped in to ease the tension. 'Relax, Krishna. It's just red tape.' He patted him on the shoulder. Petra noticed how Ed carried himself with self-assurance and an air of seniority, like the calm commanding officer welcoming visitors to his barracks. He explained to the group, 'It takes

Hector ages to fill out a multitude of forms. These tunnels are still jointly owned by the Gibraltar government and the British military, hence … paperwork. Part of what we pay him for is to be getting on with all that while you're enjoying the tour.' He took the stack of scanned passports and, glancing at each photo page, returned them to their owners.

'So if you'd all like to follow me,' said Mary, and started into the gloom.

'Wait!' shouted Krishna, and there was a sigh from the rest of the group.

'What now?' asked Carly.

'I need a picture!'

Dane groaned as they gathered in a group while Krishna extended his futuristic selfie-stick, all black carbon fibre and brushed alloy, and lifted a wobbling smart-phone high above them.

'Smile,' grinned Krishna.

'Eyes and teeth,' smiled Mary, and the phone emitted a satisfying shutter-click. 'All right! Let's go inside the Rock of Gibraltar!'

Carly made a little whooping sound that sounded more pitiful than she'd intended, and Dane laughed. Within a few short steps into the cavernous mouth of the tunnel, everything changed.

Three

First it was the smell. Just a few steps into the gloom, the summer scents of flowering shrubs and salty ocean were beaten back by the heavy funk of old cellars and damp walls. Carly crumpled her nose a little as they trod further into the oppressive greyness. The afternoon daylight retreated from their backs as the group walked into a carved tunnel more than twice their height and as wide as a country road. Ahead of them the wall was strung with dim electric lights, the yellow bulbs illuminating little more than the rugged sheen of the black walls around them.

'Welcome *inside* Gibraltar,' announced Ed holding his arms wide. Petra noticed he walked with a slight limp. 'We're inside what we on Gib call the World War Two tunnels, but they've actually been around far longer. They're an extension of the great siege tunnels of 1779. They weren't fully excavated by the British army until 1939. Seventy years ago it would've been my comrades in the Royal Engineers who completed the incredible engineering task around you.'

That explains the officer swagger, thought Petra. Ex military.

'Sappers. The branch of the army that does all the manual work – like digging.' He turned to face the darkness ahead of them and raised his voice. 'Over thirty miles of tunnels!'

He walked onwards and Dane asked, 'Thirty miles? How big is Gibraltar?'

'Cool fact, actually,' Mary replied. 'Gib is only two point six square miles, but this tunnel network runs to *thirty-four* miles of twists, turns, tangles and drops. Everything from huge tunnels like this, which was cut large enough to drive a truck down, to tiny crawl spaces.'

Petra looked back and the light from outside was long gone, defeated by the damp, black walls of the last couple of turns they'd made. The dim yellow light from the string of bulbs gave each of them a pallid complexion. Even Carly's spray-tan looked washed out.

'It's all hollow, this place we call home,' Ed continued from the front of the pack. 'Very pretty on the outside, but a cavernous, empty space within.'

'Like Carly's head,' Krishna quipped, which got a laugh from Dane, swiftly halted with a dig in the ribs from his fiancée.

Their jocular mood and slightly nervous giggling continued for a few more minutes while Ed and Mary pointed out various features on their journey: ventilation grilles and iron drainage grids, tool marks on the rock walls made by the soldiers, many of them former miners, who'd hacked this natural fortress from within the Earth. Dark, lonely and devoid of life, it seemed to Petra the exact opposite to the vibrant jungles or forests she'd have chosen to explore. Weird thing for Krishna to have chosen. That probably said quite a lot about Krishna. Besides, right now she'd take almost anything over moping in her crumby post-break-up bed-sit.

And what of this couple, Ed and Mary? Married? Boyfriend and girlfriend? As Petra watched Ed talking, the dim lights sparking an occasional twinkle in his eyes, a hint of old-public-school accent, the assured stride with the slight limp, she envied Mary. Just slightly. They seemed perfectly lovely, far too normal to be making a living this way, and Petra was just about to satisfy her curiosity by asking them how they'd ended up here when they rounded a corner into a huge cavern that drew gasps and *aahs* from the visitors.

Unlike the hand-hewn tunnels they'd just walked through, this large cave was entirely natural, lined with hundreds of stalactites above a large pool of water. What nature had turned into an acoustic bowl, humans had turned into an auditorium. There was raked seating down one side, a stage cut into the rock on the other side of the pool, and the entire space was tastefully lit with green, blue and orange splashes of light. Multicoloured reflections shimmered on the surface of the water, making shadows around the stalactites dance silently above.

'Welcome to Saint Michael's cave,' said Ed. 'The most famous place inside the rock.' Krishna was making 'whoop' noises to hear the reverberations bounce around, but Ed pressed on. 'As you can see, these days it's used as a concert venue, partly, as Krishna has discovered, because of its incredible acoustics.'

'Sound travels a long way inside the rock due to the hard stone surfaces,' explained Mary. 'It can be quite unsettling. Sometimes when you're in a tunnel you hear noises and have no idea how near or far away they are.'

'The sound literally bounces around the rock. If you stand in just the right spot in here you can sometimes hear you own voice come back at you a second later. Try it, Krishna.'

Krishna cleared his throat, pulled in a chestful of air, and shouted, 'HELLO!' at the top of his voice. The resonance fell away and they all stood in silence, expectantly waiting.

After a few seconds Dane slapped him on the shoulder. 'Literally *no one* wants to talk to you.'

'When they were digging these tunnels during the Second World War they found a much larger freshwater lake, deep in the middle of the rock, even lower than this,' Ed explained. 'That's harder to get to. The further down you go, the more inaccessible the tunnels. In fact most of the tunnels in this rock are below us but the lower levels were sealed off by the military years ago. Too dangerous.'

'But we can still take you to our favourite place,' Mary said, heading out of the beautifully lit cavern into another dark tunnel. They dutifully followed and found themselves in more cramped space, certainly too small for any truck. Petra stretched out her arms and could touch the walls either side. The rock felt cold and slippery. The crocodile of explorers crept through an opening where a huge steel door, brown with rust, hung on massive hinges driven into the rock.

'Mind your fingers,' said Ed. 'This is a blast-trap. These doors were fitted during the Second World War.' He pointed up to the ridge cut into the stone where the door would close. 'See? They only open one way. If there's an explosion, a bomb dropping outside, the force of the blast pushes the steel door against the rock and is diverted into here.' He gestured off to the side and Dane and Carly poked their heads around the smooth pillar of a corner. Carly gave an unimpressed grunt and Krishna and Petra pushed themselves past to see a large, hollowed-out cave, the shape of a mushroom lying on its side. 'The theory being that the blast is trapped here and on the other side of the door you're safe.'

'Did that really work?' Dane scoffed.

'It was never tested. Gib was never attacked.'

'What's this?' Krishna picked up a clear plastic

31

tube with some liquid in it.

'The place is littered with these. The military boys used glow-sticks during their exercises back in the nineties.'

'The lighting down here gets pretty poor,' Mary said, slipping off her backpack. 'So if it was good enough for them …' She handed a few glow-sticks out to each of them. 'Just one of the perks of Ed's forces contacts,' she said with a smile. 'I've got a few torches, plus you can use your phones, but if you need it, bend the tube until you hear a crack, it'll glow for about an hour. Just in case you get separated or lost. Here you go.' She handed Dane and Petra a torch each and grabbed the last one from her bag for herself.

The final attraction on the tour was the most macabre. After five minutes of treading carefully along black, uneven floors, their torch beams sweeping along layers of wet, craggy walls, occasionally striped with green or black stripes of sedimentary rock, they turned sharp left and Petra could tell by the change in acoustics that they had entered a large room.

'Hold on a second. There's lots to trip you up in here and I don't want you to get hurt.' Ed walked away from them and Petra heard a large switch click before a battered fluorescent strip-light arced into life. There were gasps and '*woah*'s as their eyes adjusted to the buzzing yellow glow. They were standing at one end of a long, rectangular hospital ward. Eight rusting bed frames formed two neat rows on either side. The space was cluttered with decrepit IV stands, broken metal drawers and rotting steel cupboards slumped drunkenly on broken wheels. The air felt cold and Petra smelled the metallic tang of rust in the atmosphere.

'This hospital was built in 1940. During the war thousands of British troops lived and worked inside the Rock. Under a full-scale attack they could have survived in here for years.'

'Gross,' murmured Carly. 'This is disgusting.'

'This is awesome!' said Krishna, extending his phone to arm's length to start filming. 'It's gonna look amazing!'

'Put your phone away, dude. It's too dark.'

'Oh, Dane,' Krishna said. 'So naïve. It's got *night-vision!* He listed its assets while sweeping it slowly across the scene. 'Shockproof, waterproof, voice recognition and 4K picture quality.'

'Very impressive,' Mary agreed. 'And can it be used as a telephone?'

This got a chuckle from the group and Dane

33

said, 'He wouldn't know. No one ever calls him.'

'Not true, someone tried to sell me life insurance only this morning,' Krishna shot back, keeping his eye on the green, night-vision image on his screen.

'Did soldiers … die in here?' Carly asked.

'Certainly,' said Mary. 'Thousands lived inside the Rock so like any town there was sickness, injury, death. Take a look in here.' She led them across the room to a black rectangular opening at the far end. Carly hesitated at the threshold. 'Go on,' urged Mary.

Petra saw in the torchlight rows of hollowed-out shelves in the walls, like those in a church crypt. Their dimensions meant only one thing. 'The morgue.'

'Correct!' grinned Mary, delighted. 'These might only have been used if they were under siege.' She stroked her hand along one of the hollowed out morgue slabs. 'But I love them. Aren't they great?'

'Fuck that,' grunted Carly, and reversed back out.

Ed led them back along the ward and as he stepped forward he stumbled slightly. Mary reached out to support him and Petra heard him mutter 'Bloody leg' under his breath. She felt a flutter. Sympathy? Attraction? Emotionally she

34

was all over the place since breaking up with Zach. She dismissed the fleeting feeling and concentrated on the morbid space around her.

'This is horrible,' Carly said, hugging herself to avoid touching anything else.

'Really?' smiled Ed. 'I love it.'

'Weirdo,' muttered Krishna.

'I do! It's probably our medical background.'

'We both studied medicine at uni,' Mary explained, placing her hand in Ed's.

'You're doctors?' asked Petra. Could this guy be any more remarkable? Ex-military, good looking *and* a doctor?

'Not exactly. I trained to be a nurse. Ed's the high flyer. Biomedical Sciences, chemistry, medical research and all that.'

'You're kidding! I did Biomed at Warwick.' At last, she was in her comfort zone. 'Where did you study?'

'Durham,' Mary replied for him. The pride in her voice felt a little defensive, a barbed declaration of status to put Petra in her place.

'Were you any good?' asked Dane, idly examining a half-open rusty drawer.

Carly tutted and whispered, 'It's not a competition, darlin'.'

Ed just smiled. 'I was OK.'

'He was a genius,' Mary affirmed, squeezing Ed's hand. 'Won the Medawar Innovation Grant. Only one person a year gets that.'

'So how come you're down here, with us?' asked Dane.

Carly rolled her eyes; Petra wondered at what point Dane's alpha-male competitiveness went from being quite attractive to a bit tiresome.

'We … had a difference of opinion,' Ed explained, 'the professors and me. I walked away.'

The confidence Petra had noticed in Ed earlier bordered on arrogance as the men puffed their chests. 'To this?' she asked. It sounded ruder than she'd expected and Mary showed a flash of daggers in her glance. 'Sorry, I didn't mean …'

Ed smiled. 'It's fine. It must seem strange. It was some mates in the Medical Corps that introduced me to Gibraltar, and I was smitten. I persuaded Mary to join me out here a-sap. She still holds me responsible for ruining her studies!'

'Your parents can't have been too happy about that,' Petra said, unable to stop digging.

'My parents aren't around any more.'

'I was thinking about yours!' Petra said to Mary.

'Both our parents are no longer with us,' she

replied with a steely directness that belied her soft features. The atmosphere had got awkward.

Carly perked up, blatantly changing the subject. 'This has been lovely. Can we go?'

Four

Within moments they were shuffling out of the dingy, rotting infirmary along another damp grey tunnel. Petra felt a pull on her sleeve. It was Carly, tugging at her to hang back from the group.

'What the fuck?'

'What?' whispered Petra.

'What was all that? Why are you being weird?'

I'm weird?'

'Well, it's hardly going to impress Krishna, having a go at them two. This was his idea.'

'Wait, what? Why would I want to impress Krishna?'

'Oh come on, Petra.' Carly smirked, and then

whispered in a sing-song voice, 'I think he likes you.'

'Oh, pur-*lease,*' scowled Petra, shaking her head. She marched on to catch the others, leaving Carly trotting after her, muffled giggles resonating around them. This labyrinth was losing its charm. Ahead, Ed had stopped at a large, rusted gate adorned with signs in English and Spanish that clearly indicated that the path beyond it was out of bounds. 'This is the end of the road,' he said. 'Well, for us it is.'

Great, thought Petra. *Let's get out of here.*

'Most of the inner network and the entire lower galleries are still owned by the military,' said Mary. Petra was unsettled by how quickly Mary had returned to her smiling, helpful self after the fierce glance she had shot her moments ago.

'Shall we go, then?' suggested Petra.

'What's through there?' asked Dane.

'Prohibited,' said Ed.

Dane peered through the bars into the blackness beyond and muttered something about health and safety and a nanny state. Petra was watching Krishna film through the barred gate on his phone. The screen looked like a smudgy green smear from where she was, but he persisted on fiddling with settings, lost in his own world. She raised an eyebrow to Carly as they watched, which she hoped said, 'Really? Him?' and Carly just smirked and whispered: 'Nerd.'

The tour all but finished, they were back in the wider tunnels dimly illuminated with electric bulbs when Carly gasped. 'Ohhhhh my God, *look!*'

In a gloomy alcove cut into the wall at shoulder height sat a large black ape, squatting like a statue. At its feet a young ape idly picked at the fur of its mother.

Petra's heart leapt. She'd seen these monkeys at a distance when they were walking up the path outside, but to be just a few metres from one was breathtaking.

'The Barbary macaques,' said Ed. 'A species of monkey known locally as the rock ape.'

'Adorable!' cooed Carly.

'Bloody pain,' Ed replied. 'Always pestering tourists in the hope of stealing food.'

'Good luck getting any food off Krishna,' said Dane, but Krishna was too busy fiddling with his phone settings to respond.

'Oh, don't mind old grumpy-pants,' smiled Mary. 'The novelty's worn off for us, but they are quite cute. Cute, but bad-tempered.'

'If you see a plastic snake in a car in Gib, this is why. The rock apes have become so used to humans they're fearless. They'll steal bags, wallets, phones, but they still run away from a fake snake.'

'Just wait a minute while I capture this,' Krishna said, framing his shot.

While they waited for the budding camerman, Mary turned to Carly. 'So, congratulations are in order. Can I see the ring?'

'Ahh, thanks, hun!' Carly beamed and spread her manicured left hand for inspection.

'Oh, it's beautiful!' Mary shone her torch at the sparkling ring and said, 'Isn't it, Ed?'

'What's that?'

'Beautiful. Carly's engagement ring.'

'Sure. Congratulations.'

'Imagine how a girl must feel to be given one of these.'

Ed just smirked.

'I don't suppose …?' she asked Carly. 'No, sorry, that's unprofessional of me.'

'What? You wanna try it on? Please, take it! Never know, he might like the look of it, give him some inspiration!' She smiled at Ed and slid off the ring. Mary held it under the torchlight, captivated.

'Just a bit of video,' Krishna murmured, gazing

41

at his phone screen.

'Hurry up, mate,' Dane sighed.

As Krishna crabbed, knees bent, tracking his phone camera towards the apes, he said, 'Eat your heart out, David Attenborough,' which made Petra smile.

Then Dane said, 'Go on mate, get your big close-up,' and planted his knee in Krishna's protruding bottom. He stumbled forwards and a deafening shriek filled their ears.

Before anyone could react, a dark shape erupted from the alcove and engulfed Krishna. Everyone yelled, and clattered into each other as they lurched back. As the swinging beam from Ed's torch sliced the gloom, Petra saw muscular black fur clamped around Krishna's head. She pushed herself against the wall, deafening shouts rattling off rock, and saw the light settle on the rock ape that was clinging to Krishna as he flailed and spun. The monkey's teeth were bared, it bore a white blaze across its head, and she was shocked to see a twitching black stump where it was missing an arm.

Krishna's flapping limbs failed to shake off the beast, whose good arm was firmly anchored around his neck. Still yelling, he found the selfie-

42

stick in his pocket and swiped above him. The ape expertly dodged the extended stick and leapt clear while Krishna kept whipping and swiping at the floor, the walls, every hard surface, hopelessly missing his attacker. Petra, like her friends, gathered her breath and watched as Krishna's gyrating chaos slowly subsided. Even the ape, she noticed, sat and watched as its baby sauntered from the alcove to take a seat. Eventually, their panting friend stopped for breath and looked at the remnant in his hand – an alloy handle sprouting tatty, splintered strands of plastic.

Ed shooed the animal away without a second thought, and the monkey didn't protest. 'Sorry about that. Camera shy, clearly.'

Relief swept the gang into laughter, apart from Krishna, who looked decidedly pissed off.

'Aww,' said Petra. 'Did you see she only had one arm, poor thing.'

'Pests!' shouted Ed. 'Could have hurt someone.' Then added, 'And the ape could've done some damage, too,' which got another ripple of laughter from the group.

Petra felt a little sympathy for Krishna, standing forlorn, sweating, examining the shredded plastic in his hand. Dane leaned close and said, 'Mate, I think your selfie-stick's broken,' but before Krishna could react Mary swore.

She was holding her hand up in front of her face. 'Oh my God! The ring! Where's the ring?'

'What?' demanded Carly.

'Your engagement ring?' Dane asked.

'It was on my finger, I swear. Then I got bumped, and … shit.' Mary started scanning the floor around their feet.

'Why did you take it off, Carly?' Dane asked.

'Why did you shove Krishna into the monkey, *Dane?*'

'Guys, c'mon,' Petra said. 'It'll be here somewhere.'

But six pairs of eyes saw nothing under the sweeping torch beams. No glint of gold or jewelled spark, just craggy, slippery limestone.

'Are you sure you lost it here?' asked Ed.

'Yes! It was on my finger just now,' barked Mary, 'right before that fucking monkey jumped out!'

Petra joined Carly, crouching, gently sweeping the damp ground with her fingers.

'I'm so sorry,' Mary said, widening her search. She and Ed went in one direction, crouching, inspecting every bump and ridge while Petra extended her own search area.

'It's gotta be here somewhere.'

'It was a massive jump, though – I mean, I nearly hit the roof,' Carly replied. Dane stayed quiet and joined her, squatting down, checking the ground with his fingertips.

After a few moments of silent, fruitless searching, Mary said, 'Er … guys.' Petra looked up to see her and Ed standing a short distance away. Mary was pointing at the ground. They gathered around, all of them looking down, not at an expensive diamond ring, but at a grimy iron grid. 'You don't think …?'

'You've got to be kidding me,' said Dane, sounding as gloomy as their surroundings.

'What's down there?' asked Carly.

'The lower tunnels,' said Ed. 'All sealed off. Out of bounds. I hope you had insurance, Dane.'

Carly was appalled. 'What? No way! I'm not getting some crappy replacement. That was the ring you *proposed* with, Dane. It's priceless. I'm getting it back.'

Ed wasn't keen. He explained again: the tunnels below were out of bounds for a reason: they were dangerous. Miles of twisting mazes, hidden drops, rock-falls, lakes.

'I'm out,' said Krishna.

'Helpful, mate. Thanks,' replied Dane.

'And besides,' Ed added. 'We've got to be out of here in ten minutes. The entrance gets closed and there's usually a police patrol car around the place for a while.'

'But it's just down there!' whined Carly with a little stamp of her foot.

Petra tried to ease the situation. 'Come on, Carly. We'll work something out. Let's go.' The group started walking away, up the rising slope towards the gaping mouth of the Rock that had swallowed them an hour ago, but Carly was reluctant. Still keeping her attention on the grid, she eventually tore herself away with a cry of frustration and trotted after the others.

Outside the tunnel entrance Petra drank in the twilight air, filled with the scent of wild rosemary and sea-lavender. But the mood had turned sour. Carly was trying to persuade Ed to take her down to the tunnel below the drainage grid. Petra thought he looked half-convinced, though Mary was at his ear, balancing Carly's pleas with the risks: her desire to repair her mistake versus a list of reasons why it couldn't happen – it was illegal, they could lose their business if they got caught; she even mentioned smugglers.

'*You* don't have to come,' pleaded Carly. 'Just show me the way.'

'Smugglers?' asked Petra.

Ed explained. 'This weird hollow rock is the back door into Europe for every gangster, drug dealer and crime syndicate based just a few miles over there in Africa. Believe me, you do *not* want to be inside the Rock at night.'

'Hmmm, let me think about this,' said Krishna. 'Yes. I'm definitely out.' He walked away and Dane threw his hands in the air and tutted.

'Come on, mate, really?'

'Count me out,' he said, wandering towards a bench. 'I'm not actually feeling too well. Reckon that prawn sandwich at the airport was a bit dodgy.'

Dane turned his attention to Ed. 'C'mon, Ed, what's it gonna take to fix this? A hundred? Just take us back in and we'll be done in a few minutes.' The beat of silence told Petra that something was about to change. No immediate push-back from Ed. Mary looked like she wanted to put things right, and shared an *if you will, I will* glance with her colleague, or boyfriend, or whatever the hell they were to each other. Dane's sales instincts were finely tuned and sensed victory. 'Two hundred. For half an hour of your time.'

Another pause. Then Ed put out his hand to have it clasped by Dane, who looked like he'd negotiated the deal of his life. 'Fine,' Ed said.

Petra was suddenly struck with an uncomfortable thought. 'Are we *all* going back in?'

'Better if it's just Dane and Carly. It's not really a tourist attraction down there.'

'Ahh, what?' complained Carly.

'The more eyes the better, surely,' Dane replied, and Petra slumped slightly.

'It'll be quicker and safer with just the two of you,' Mary said. 'And it looks like Krishna's not keen.' He'd plonked himself on the seat and was playing with his phone.

'Just let me shut up shop,' said Ed. 'You two wait here and we'll be back in a couple of minutes. We'll have to use another way in.'

Mary folded the small wooden table where Hector had sat, picked up the chair and followed Ed back into the tunnel where he was switching off lights and pulling at stubborn gates.

Petra felt Carly grip her hand. 'Oh pleeeease,' she whined, looking up at her. They were eleven years old again and Petra was about to be led into some naughty escapade by her firecracker friend.

Petra shouted to the slumped figure on the bench, 'What about you, Krishna?'

'Think I'll head back,' he hollered. 'Got a ticking clock on an online mission with a gamer in Ohio.' She rolled her eyes. Was her life destined to be spent surrounded by gamer geeks? She looked at Carly and sighed, which was all Carly needed.

She squealed and said, 'Love you, hun.'

Dane wandered over to Krishna to form the second arm of the recruitment campaign. 'Come on, mate, what's up?'

Krishna didn't look up from his phone screen, on which a dragon soared around a flaming castle as he tipped the phone like a steering wheel. 'Honestly,' he said, 'I don't feel well.'

'You need to man up, buddy. How d'you think you're going to impress Petra? I think you might be in, there.'

'Oh yeah, I'm sure she was really impressed when that monkey made me nearly shit myself.'

Dane suppressed a laugh. 'Dude, this whole trip was like … a double date. Finally, a decent chance for you to get a girlfriend – Petra is Carly's weirdest friend. If you can't get off with her, then … well, you might as well cut it off, let it fend for

49

itself.' They both glanced at Krishna's crotch but Dane's smirk was only met with a heavy sigh from his friend.

'I'll see you back at the hotel.' Krishna walked away without another word, leaving Dane shaking his head and shrugging to Petra and Carly. As he wandered back to join them, Petra heard her name on the breeze.

'Petra!' The whisper was from behind them, beyond the thorny shrubs and bushes. 'Petra!' She walked towards the voice and saw, crouching below them, Ed, on a lower outcrop of shale and rock. 'Quickly!'

She gestured to Dane and Carly and the three of them clambered down the short slope to join their military commander. They were on a narrow pathway that snaked its way around the curve of the rock about three metres below the wider road above. A silhouette appeared from round the corner: Mary, effortlessly cat-walking along the ridge. It seemed a needlessly over-confident way to join them, Petra thought. Who was she trying to impress? Immediately their attention was grabbed by the sound of a car approaching. Peering up, they saw first the bumper, the bonnet, and then, as it swung slowly round, the unmistakable paintwork of a police car.

Instinctively they all squatted a little lower. The patrol car scrunched slowly in front of the tunnel and pulled up facing the dark mouth of the gated entrance. Its side windows were clearly visible to the perching trespassers, so they squatted out of sight.

'Don't worry,' Ed whispered. 'They don't usually stay.'

As if on cue, the engine was switched off. Petra arched an eyebrow at Ed. 'You were saying?'

'Just sit tight,' he assured them, and as he said that they heard the car door open, just five or six metres away from them, followed by the crunch of boots on gravel. 'C'mon. Let's go.'

As they started down the narrow ridge, Carly lost her footing and sent a shower of loose shale bouncing down below them. She clutched Dane's hand and gasped. 'Shit. Sorry. No harm done.' But from above them Petra heard a voice say something in Spanish.

'Quickly!' urged Ed, and they crept onwards on near-silent feet down the slope to an old wrought iron gate in the side of the rock. It opened inwards and was ajar just enough for Ed to squeeze through without brushing against it.

'Follow me. And be quiet.'

Mary slid expertly through and Petra found herself next. She wasn't as lithe as Mary but was proud of her dexterity in slipping silently through the gap. Then the smell hit her. Ed had led them into the vilest squatters' den, a cramped cave ankle deep in detritus left by past visitors: rank litter, bottles, crushed cans. Disturbing it sent a few flies up around her, and swatting them away from her face Petra wondered if this was the worst two hundred quid anyone had ever spent. Carly was eying up the rusty gate, her mouth twisted into a grimace. Behind her Dane sensed her unease and reached forward to open the gate a little wider. It made a loud scraping squeak as it battled with the debris and centuries of rust in its hinges.

'Who's there?' came a voice from above.

Ed hushed them and beckoned Carly and Dane into the hiding place. Just beyond the gate, a torch beam swung through the grey light from on high.

Five

To Petra it felt like hours but was only a couple of minutes, standing like statues, static human figurines frozen in a theatre of shit. She tried to hold her breath but her lungs ached, so she allowed herself shallow breathing through her mouth. Even holding her nose didn't stop the stench hitting the back of her throat. Dane had pulled his T-shirt up over his nose, but it didn't appear to be helping him either. All it did was expose his ripped stomach, enticing Carly to place her hand there, a subconscious instinct. The searchlight torch from above vanished and Ed said, 'He's not coming down.'

'Think we got away with that,' Mary said, relaxing her breathing.

'Sorry about the gate,' Dane said.

'Last of the great cat burglars,' said Petra.

'Oi,' Carly protested. 'That was chivalry.' She stroked Dane's torso, tugged his T-shirt from his face and kissed him on the lips.

'Really?' asked Petra. 'Here?' Her schoolmate had lost none of her incorrigible sexuality. She turned to Ed. 'What happened to "They don't usually stay?"'

'Just bad luck. If they've heard a rumour about smugglers or whatever, they occasionally plonk an officer up here for the night. Partly as a deterrent, but mainly because it's a good lookout spot.'

Petra looked cautiously through the bars of the gate. 'Hey it's fine,' Mary reassured them. 'He's gone.'

'We can get to the tunnels through here,' said Ed. 'This area is below where you lost your ring. But let's close this. If our friend up there comes snooping, we'll hear him.' He moved past them towards the heavy gate and lifted it on its hinges to start quietly swinging it closed. For a man with an injured leg, he was very strong.

Petra saw her chance of freedom slipping away.

'Wait. This is … too much. I think I should go.'

Ed paused, resting the gate on the ground again. 'Absolutely, you should go back if you're not sure.'

'What? No!' complained Carly.

'I mean, I *want* to help, Carly, but –'

'Oh come on, Petra. The more of us the better. Just come with us. We won't be in here long.'

'I don't like it, Carls. I wish I'd gone back to the hotel with Krishna.'

'You still can,' said Mary, gesturing towards the open gate. 'Look, why don't you get Krishna and go over the border to the tapas bar we were telling you about? The crossing won't be busy; you'll be there in half an hour. We've all got our passports. When we've found Carly's ring we'll all walk over and we can show them where you are.'

This sounded tempting, and even as Petra was weighing up a potentially awkward hour alone with Krishna versus the grotty hole she was standing in, her friend clasped her hand.

'Please come and help,' Carly said with pleading eyes.

'I'll text you the details of the bar while we've got a signal,' Mary said to Petra, ignoring Carly and tapping on her phone. 'Once you're in here you'll be cut off.'

Torn between the two worlds, the fresh, fragrant night air and this rancid stink, torn between freedom and duty, Petra slumped her shoulders and submitted to the weight of duty. Carly gave a tiny clap of her hands, Ed and Mary shrugged to each other, and Ed hoisted the gate closed.

That was when Petra noticed something odd. As the iron frame of the gate met the stone wall, she saw that it was bent, creased against the lip of solid rock. 'Jesus, look at that. Someone's tried to *push* their way out of here.'

Dane peered closer. 'Blimey, that's taken some force.'

Ed seemed less interested. 'Some local delinquent struggling with the complexities of push versus pull!'

'Or tried to leave in a hurry,' Petra whispered, running her fingers over the distorted, pitted hulk of metal.

Ed stomped his way through the trash, his lopsided limp sending crisp wrappers and food cartons scattering, and Mary said, 'Probably just vandals. Bored kids, wouldn't you say, Ed? This place is full of them. Watch out for needles.'

'That's really gross, can we get going?' Carly asked.

Ed led the way, stooping into the dark, narrowing

funnel of the cave, followed by Mary, then Dane holding Carly's hand, and Petra at the rear. But before they'd got more than a few paces Carly halted them. With whispers of *Wait!* and *What?* the line stopped moving. 'I saw it! I saw something!' Carly ordered Mary to point the torch towards the floor near her feet and started picking at the litter, cautiously lifting detritus between finger and thumb.

They watched the circle of white light with growing disgust as Carly pulled litter – most of it damp, mouldy and unrecognisable – from the ground. She recoiled when she plucked a spent condom from the crater of filth. 'Ewwww, not even *I* would …'

'Shit, Carly, what are you doing?' demanded Dane.

'I'm telling you, I saw a glint. A sparkle. It was … HA!' Victorious, she pulled something up into the light. 'Oh.' Rather than her ring, she'd discovered a silver crucifix on a silver chain.

Petra crouched next to her to examine the find. 'This chain has been snapped.' But before her thoughts could continue, she was interrupted by a squeal from Carly, who leapt to her feet. She clasped onto Dane and pointed at the ground.

'What? What now?' he asked.

Ed turned on his torch to bathe the fetid carpet in more light. Petra gasped as she glimpsed the cause of Carly's shock. In the small hole Carly had excavated, buried under the damp rubbish, the light of the torches caught the dirty sheen of a fingernail on the tip of a finger. Petra swore.

'What *is* that?' Ed asked, leaning closer. Dane used the toe of his trainer to push aside the surrounding waste, revealing a small, sallow, waxy hand. Carly gagged and pulled Dane away.

The morbid reality struck Petra. 'Is it … a body?'

Dane said, 'Oh God, a kid.' Carly coughed, a rasp of vomit scorching her throat.

Mary stooped forward and swept an armful of crap aside to disclose not a dead child at all, but a dead ape. Petra breathed a huge sigh of relief and heard Dane whisper *'Thank Christ'* under his breath. The revulsion she'd felt a moment ago was replaced with a swell of sympathy within her. She crouched back down and stroked the creature's matted fur. 'Poor thing. What happened to you?'

Carly was still emitting claggy throat retches, but Dane, now fully composed, said, 'You are properly weird, Petra.'

With a tenderness at odds with their surroundings, Petra gently pulled away the fallen animal's shroud of forgotten plastic and paper. Almost immediately she lurched back in surprise. The torch beam showed that the ape was missing a leg. In its place was a mangled stump crawling with maggots, a spot-lit glow of writhing life in a pit of death. This was the final straw for Carly, who staggered away in search of purer air. Petra wasn't horrified, but was mystified. 'What would do that?'

'Animals,' suggested Mary. 'A dog, maybe?'

'Probably already injured,' Ed mused, looking at the sorry beast. 'Crawled in here to die. That's a good meal for a fox.'

'Can we *please* find my ring!' pleaded Carly from behind them, almost at the point of tears.

'Roger that.' Ed resumed his commander resolve. 'Follow me. Just through here.' He disappeared under a low ridge. 'Stay close. And stay left. No tourist walkways here. There's a nasty drop to the right.'

Petra's feet were heavy. She was gnawed at by unanswered questions and sluggish with regret for not being strong enough to leave when she had the chance. As her friends stooped into the passage-

59

way, consumed by gloom, she dragged herself through the sad stench of the ape-grave and onward into an unknown darkness.

Six

Krishna's friendship with Dane was full of moments like this. They'd met at the logistics company when they both went through the induction course at the same time. Krishna got a job there straight from Harlow College whereas Dane was a year older and already had a heap of sales experience before joining Armpro. Dane was senior, good-looking and responsible for managing a small team. Krishna was none of those. Despite them joining the firm on the same day, Krishna felt like the new boy every time he was with Dane at work.

Thankfully, that wasn't often. Krishna worked

in data processing, number-crunching at a desk all day. Dane worked on a different floor, wooing new clients and trying not to lose the existing ones, and was within reach of a company BMW and a corner office. By and large their friendship worked. It had changed, of course. In almost four years it had gone from regular nights on the beer plus football at the weekend to fewer drunken nights and only meeting up for cup matches or international games. They'd even flat-shared for a year, but that was before Carly. For a guy driven by status symbols, Carly had been the perfect catch: vivacious, curvy, blonde, she was straight out of the pages of one of Dane's lad mags.

And now they were engaged. Krishna hadn't see that coming. Although the more he'd got to know Carly, the more he'd suspected that beneath the party girl façade was a woman who yearned for some grounded commitment; so maybe he shouldn't have been too surprised.

As he trudged slowly back into the town of Gibraltar, Krishna reflected on how this feeling of being the outcast was not unfamiliar. Worse, it was a pattern. Ever since he'd known Dane there had been evenings like this. Bilzy's stag do sprang to mind. A dozen blokes in Belarus, of all places, and whose suitcase didn't turn up? Krishna spent two hours filling in forms at the airport while the rest of them charged into the cold Minsk air for a hot night of vodka-fuelled debauchery. The England game in Marseille. Three weeks' wages went on that trip, and where was Krishna when Dier scored England's only goal? Fetching burgers for the boys. And worse, it was a 1-1 draw. Against *Russia!*

There was a twisted logic to it, an equation in Krishna's mathematical mind: Krishna + Dane + highly emotive environment = Dane has a great time while Krishna looks like a tit. Apparently, being on this peculiar rock made no difference to the immovable maths of their friendship. Descending a flight of steps into the warm lights of the town centre, he shrugged off his insecurities and headed towards the hotel. What had seemed like a cheap B&B pub in the daylight took on a more welcoming character after dark. The Luna Rossa Hotel, casting its faded-amber light over the cobbled street, was little more than a bar with some rooms above it, but thanks to recently putting the word 'boutique' in front of 'hotel' on their TripAdvisor listing, they were rarely without guests. Krishna liked the place but detected that their arrival that morning had been a disappointment to Carly and Petra. Girls were like that. Always making a mountain out of a shower curtain.

At the door he paused at a parish noticeboard, a scuffed Perspex window into another world: meat raffles, whist drives, a poster declaring 'Desaparecidos' above a picture of a pretty girl. Written in Spanish, it looked like the girl (age twenty-three, Krishna deciphered) had gone missing. The rudimentary details described red hair and a tattoo. Alongside her smiling picture was a close-up of a tattoo: Disney's Tigger, grinning in blue ink. Judging by the poster's crusty, curled corners this was not a recent story. Half pasted across it was a flyer for 'Madame Rosella', whose services ranged from tarot-card readings to full-immersion spirit-guide séances. She also did pedicures.

The Luna Rossa's thick wooden door, held together by centuries of gloss paint, led to a small hallway not big enough to do anything but make a choice: two frosted glass doors offered *Hotel* on the right, or opposite, *Bar*. Krishna turned left.

He walked into a room filled with chatter, cigarette smoke and … men. That was the first thing he noticed, the lack of women and the abundance of smoke. In England smoking in public buildings had been banned for years. It was why most of Krishna's colleagues 'vaped'. Puffing on electronic cigarettes still allowed them to take regular breaks from their workstations. This bar was like a nicotine-coloured slice of a forgotten era: a 1970s working men's club, wrenched from a sodden working-class backstreet and dropped among the lapping waves of the Mediterranean. A handful of locals sat at sticky tables playing dominoes, dealing cards, or laughing at a yellowing wall-mounted TV showing a home-video calamities show.

A barman wiped some glasses, staring at the screen. Krishna perched on a stool, and the man – tanned, craggy, with neatly cropped hair – put down his cloth and smiled a crooked 'what can I get you?' smile. Krishna placed a fifty-euro note on the bar and said, 'Una cerveza, por favor.'

The barman raised his eyebrows and said, in a soft Scottish accent straight out of Perthshire, 'And what sorta beer d'you want?'

Trying to style out his misinterpretation of the mahogany man's origins, Krishna surveyed the beer pumps as if choosing a fine wine. 'I'll … take … a … lager. Pint.'

The barman flicked a plastic tap and familiar golden beer frothed in a glass. As he slid it to Krishna, the barman held up the orange euro note and said, 'I'll take it, pal, but it's the Queen's sterling here.'

'Oh, really? Bloody hell, I've got three hundred in euros. Just assumed 'cause I was on my holidays it'd be euros all the way.'

'Aye, you're not the first. Where you from?'

'Basildon. In –'

'Essex. Yeah, I know it. Well, you're over a thousand miles from Basildon, laddy, but this is still England's green and pleasant land.' He stuffed the note in the cash register and slammed shut the cash drawer. 'I'll just keep it safe in there in case you want another.' With that, the perpetrator of this extortion extended his hand. 'I'm Fraser. Welcome to the Luna Rossa. My wife checked you and your friends in this morning, is that right?'

'Oh, yeah, I'm Krishna.' He felt the steel grip of Fraser's rough hand and noticed that his tight-fitting T-shirt bore a military logo beneath which were embroidered the words OP TELIC 2003. 'You, er, both run this place, then? S'lovely.'

'Aye, thirteen years.' The tone of his voice was factual. Friendly, yet at the same time without warmth. His short-cropped hair, creased, weathered face and well-toned arms made him look like a battle-worn army veteran. And that's when Krishna realised that was exactly what he was. He supped his brew and searched for a subject change.

'So let me get this straight. You've got pounds, not euros.'

'Correct.'

'Red telephone boxes like in olden days.'

'Aye.'

'There's a Marks and Spencer's.'

'Be uncivilised not to.'

'And also like the olden days, everyone's smoking in the pub and … and the whole place is crawling with mad monkeys!' Fraser laughed with a smoker's rattle. 'You've met the natives!'

'Mmm,' nodded Krishna through a slurp of froth. 'A little too closely. One of them nearly had me earlier.'

'If you think the monkeys are mad,' drawled Fraser, pouring himself a tot of whisky, 'you should meet the locals.' He pointed to a poster behind the bar and said, 'This isnae England, pal. You're on the Rock, now!' The poster had the words *THIS IS NOT ENGLAND* across the top and detailed a host of different emergency phone numbers for police, coastguard and the like. This strange welcome to a holiday destination that was never even Krishna's idea reminded him of the welcome extended by the surly drinkers of the Slaughtered Lamb in *American Werewolf in London*. He frowned at his drink and muttered, 'TripAdvisor never mentioned homicidal monkeys.'

Seven

Being inside this black, damp labyrinth was a bullet-list of wrongs for Petra. She listed them in her head while her friends, sheep-like, followed their leader.

They were breaking the law. That was one. But she'd have expected that from Carly. Carly had always viewed rules, from school attendance to taxing her car, as something more like 'guidelines'. But Petra was honest. And this was the first time she could ever remember trespassing. The fact that a policeman had shouted at them only cemented the fact that what she was doing was probably illegal.

It could cost Ed and Mary their business. She cared less about that. She'd already decided that she didn't like Mary much. It was hard to say why. She worshipped Ed, that much was clear, but something about her wasn't ... genuine? Authentic? She wasn't sure, it was just a feeling. But worse than both of those things, what the hell were they doing here in the first place? No engagement ring was worth angry cops, piles of shit and an ape's rotting corpse.

'Carly?' she called. 'Why are we doing this?'

'What d'ya mean?' the voice echoed back.

'Well, I was just thinking. Is it really worth it?'

Petra heard Mary mutter to Ed, 'You gave her a chance to leave,' which confirmed she was a bitch.

'Petra, relax,' Dane said. 'We'll be done in a few minutes. An hour from now we'll be in a bar somewhere drinking G&Ts and laughing at our adventure.'

'Quite right,' Ed agreed. He'd stopped up ahead where a sealed gate secured the mouth of another tunnel. The iron gate was cluttered with signs from different eras, riveted or tie-wrapped on, each of them indicating that the route was barred and entry was forbidden. 'We're heading through there. There's an opening round the side – but I

70

warn you, it's a bit of a squeeze.'

'Lucky we didn't bring Krishna,' Dane quipped, but nobody laughed. 'Bloody hell, where's the funeral?' he muttered, and Petra noticed how crestfallen he looked when he thought he'd said something foolish. His catalogue-model bravado was veneer thin.

Ed pulled hard at a wire-mesh fence anchored to the rock by thick industrial staples, peeling a section of it away to create a slender gap. He leaned his weight backwards and Dane led Carly through, saying a manly, 'Cheers bud,' as he passed. As Petra slid through after them she noticed tension across Ed's shoulders and arms, his white knuckles further betraying the effort involved for him. As he slid himself through after Mary, the snarling barbed edge of the thick wire mesh forced his back against the rock and snapped home behind him.

'That does not get any easier,' he panted, brushing himself down. 'How are we? All good?' The gang nodded and he resumed his position leading them into the forbidden passage. Petra kicked something that skittered under her feet. In the torchlight she saw it and picked up a spent plastic glow-tube. It still had the chemical liquid

71

inside. 'Someone's been here quite recently.'

No one seemed interested, so she dropped it and carried on behind them. After less than a minute of careful walking, the only sounds their own breathing and the occasional scuff against rock, they gathered at a dark junction. A side tunnel, the same size as theirs, maybe a couple of metres square, led off to the right.

'There are still miles of these tunnels Ed and I haven't explored,' Mary said. 'But we know *this* one very well.' She swung her torch beam up to the wall. Glistening in the bright LED beam were the words *Ed + Mary* crudely scratched into the rock, surrounded by a crooked heart.

Carly made a cooing 'Aaah' sound and Ed said, 'Bloody childish, really. Must be almost a decade since we did that.'

'Not childish!' Mary scolded. 'Adorable! I wanted the whole world to know your name and this made us both immortal. People will come from miles around to see this when you're famous.'

Ed chuckled and as Petra tracked her own torch beam across the rock she saw that Ed and Mary had not been the only subterranean visitors to leave their mark. Graffiti names and dates were scattered across the tunnel's wall, some going back as far as the 1940s. 'So much history. Why here, I wonder?'

'A junction,' Ed replied. 'Mark your junctions. Track your way out.'

'Last of the great romantics,' Mary said flatly.

'Can we just get going?' Carly's patience was now paper-thin and a history lesson was clearly not on her agenda. 'How do we get to the bit underneath that grid?'

'Of course,' said Ed. 'Just down here.'

Petra couldn't tell for sure, but after about thirty seconds she sensed Ed slowing down. Maybe his bad leg was hurting. But he also seemed to be checking his surroundings a lot more closely. When they entered a small, hollowed-out space, a room just about the size of a van, he actually did a double-check down one of the carved-out tunnel openings before nodding and choosing the tunnel opposite. With every cautious, panting step the temperature ebbed away. As did Petra's confidence.

Soon they reached a four-way junction and stopped. Mary walked a slow circle. 'Is this right, Ed? I don't recognise this bit.'

'Yeah,' he said, squinting into the dark options before them. 'Yeah – it's this way.'

Compared to the tittering group who'd hidden from the police officer just ten minutes earlier, their trepidation was palpable. The pace was slow, the air was icy, the chatter had stopped. 'God, it's so cold down here,' Petra said, almost to reassure herself that she still had a voice.

'We must be right in the middle of the rock by now,' Ed said, his voice quieter than before, authority seeping away.

'You mean … you don't *know?*' accused Carly.

Before Ed could respond they were jolted to a frozen halt by a loud crash somewhere in the distance, echoing through the arteries of the Rock.

'What the fuck was that?' demanded Carly.

'Ed?' Mary asked. She looked as unsettled as the rest.

But Ed ignored them. He was scanning the roof of their tunnel with his torch. 'That grid's got to be around here somewhere.'

Dane stepped toward him. 'Seriously mate, what *was* that?'

Ed moved onwards, his head craned back, obsessed with the rock above. 'Come on. This way.' He sped up and the others shared a glance before reluctantly following in his wake. Petra looked behind her. She could find her way back from here, she was sure of it. She watched Carly and Dane chasing Mary, swallowed in the gloom, and dragged herself after them. 'Wait for me!'

Ed's pace had picked up to almost a jog. He scanned the roof, sweeping the torch beam like a light-sabre ahead of him, cutting his way through endless black. They stopped, a breathless gaggle of adrenaline. They were at another junction. The same junction? Petra couldn't tell. Surely not. They'd been travelling straight, more or less. Hadn't they?

Ed was murmuring as he peered into the distance. 'I thought we ... wait, is it ...? I'm sure we ...'

'Are we lost?' asked Carly at almost a shriek.

'We're lost,' affirmed Petra.

'I'm sure we ...' continued Ed, but he was interrupted by a loud metallic clank, much closer than the noise a moment ago.

They all jumped and Carly clung to Dane. 'There's something in here!'

Petra's nerves were fizzing. 'Carly. I love you, you know that. But no engagement ring is worth this. Let's go back. I'm sure I can retrace our steps.'

'Yeah, you're right. But ... we must be so close, though,' she whined. 'Ed? Tell me we're close.'

After a beat of silence Dane said, 'He doesn't know where he is.'

Mary rounded on him. 'Hey! There is *no one* better to have with you right now than Ed. Don't forget who's fault it is that we're down here.'

'Er, *yours!*'

'I wouldn't have dropped the stupid ring if you hadn't shoved whatsisname.'

'*Stupid ring?*' Carly said.

Petra stepped in. 'Look, this isn't helping.'

'All I'm saying,' Mary mumbled, 'is don't bleat on about your lost ring and then have a go at the man who offered to help you find it.'

'Who was *paid* to find it,' Dane corrected.

Ed stayed silent. Tension crackled.

Petra spoke next. 'I'm going back.'

'Petra, don't cop out on me. My ring –'

'Oh for fu – *really,* Carly? Look around! We are *lost*. We're somewhere in the middle of a … a maze. Except mazes are fun. This is terrifying. This maze is cold and dark and full of death. And God knows what else! I don't know what those noises were, but right now your ring is *unimportant*. Understand? I just … want … to go!' Her eyes were infernos locked to Carly's icy glare. A hostile silence hung between them. Petra was the first to look away. With a sigh she said, 'I could have been back at the hotel with Krishna.'

Dane took command, maybe as a distraction from the squabble, and taking the torch from Carly, he grabbed her hand and said, 'This way.'

As he strode around a corner, Ed piped up. 'Dane. That's not the way. We should –'

A third loud crash boomed around them and this one was punctuated by Dane swearing. Petra heard Carly say, 'Oh my God, are you all right?' and as their torches swung round the corner she saw Dane sprawled on the ground gripping his shin. He'd tripped over something. He hobbled upright swearing through gritted teeth and the five of them stood there, three torches trained on the object languishing on the ground in the dark: a large metal box with hefty clasps and a green painted finish.

'That,' announced Ed with renewed authority, 'is an ammo box. And not a very old one, by the looks of it. Which means it belongs to someone.'

'Which means we should walk away,' Petra said.

'Which means we should open it,' replied Dane.

Mary bit her lip, looking to Ed for guidance. He said, 'If it's ammunition, I'd leave it. Nothing we can do with it anyway.'

But Dane was already on his haunches and fiddling with the clasp mechanism.

'Don't, darlin'. Let's just go.' Carly tugged at his T-shirt sleeve. 'I'm not even that bothered about my ring now. You were right. We'll get another one on the insurance.'

Petra rolled her eyes and said, 'Finally,' under her breath.

'Come on, Dane,' ordered Ed. 'The mission's changed. This is not our objective. Let's find a way out.'

As if in reply, the inanimate box jumped to life, its two latches springing open. Dane grinned and said, 'Oops.' As he pulled the metal lid open, the torchlight shone brighter, reflected back into their faces. Tightly packed into the heavy box were row upon row of polythene bags filled with bright white powder. 'Shit. You didn't tell us you were planning a party, Ed.'

Petra had never seen cocaine in real life before but had seen enough movies and schlock American TV shows to recognise this cache. As quickly as her brain could take in what she was seeing and make sense of it, she jumped. Right behind them the loud *ker-chunk* of a pistol being cocked made them all spin around. Dane leapt to his

78

feet, while out of the dark a figure moved towards them.

An eerie silhouette cast crooked shadows in the pale orange light of a paraffin lamp. In seconds he was before them, calm, chuckling, malevolent: a tall, lean man with dark skin and wiry, scrappy hair. He didn't look like a local to Petra, or even Spanish. Possibly Algerian. A bandana covered his nose and mouth but from the creases around his dark eyes Petra could tell he was smiling. He casually pointed a heavy silver pistol at Mary while he raised the lamp to get a better look at his captives. Petra, like her friends, was petrified, stuck fast. Her only movement was the shallow gasps of air from her chest. In the orange light she saw that the side of the man's face was disfigured, burned: the skin was tight and the scalp exposed.

Then, with the metallic *zing* of a large blade being drawn, she saw the second man.

Eight

Krishna wouldn't have chosen to fund a third round of drinks for him and barman-Fraser, but as the landlord was apparently also Krishna's self-appointed banker he had little choice. As foaming pint number three was pushed across the stained bar towards him, his bladder complained, giving him the excuse to take a break.

'Round the side,' instructed Fraser as Krishna slid from his high bar-stool. He followed the barman's finger towards a hallway to the side of the bar. Rounding the corner, he found himself in a cluttered, dimly lit passageway that time seemed to have forgotten, as had the cleaner. What had once been merely a sticky floor was now a slick, shiny layer of dirt-encrusted lino. Once-white gloss woodchip wallpaper had gone beyond nicotine-glazed to become mahogany-smeared and battered. With no obvious sign for the toilets Krishna stalled, sure that he'd misunderstood, and poked his head back into the bar. 'Er, where am I going?'

'Down the hall, Chris,' Fraser repeated.

Krishna was about to correct him: 'It's –' but changed his mind '– just down here, then. Great.'

He returned down the grotty hallway, and past a stack of old plastic chairs he found a door. It didn't open easily but with a grudging shove Krishna stumbled into a gloomy room. Not toilets, but a storeroom. An Aladdin's cave of crap. A broken picnic table propped against the wall, a rusty barbecue; at his feet was a broken pool cue next to a crusty grey mop. A suitcase and a couple of backpacks were plonked in the middle, and even in the smoky light bathing them from the hallway Krishna could see they were dusty. And yet the backpacks were full and the suitcase bulged. His curiosity piqued, he cocked his head to read the baggage label that was still attached to the handle. It was a faded airline tag full of barcodes and bearing the airport code GIB and a date. This luggage had been gathering dust for months.

His bladder twinged, forcing him to concentrate on his task, so he left the storeroom and realised that, thank God, there was another door further down with the word BOG written on the chipped paint in black marker pen.

Back at the bar, relieved and reinvigorated, he mentioned his mistaken diversion into the storeroom. 'I've heard of people leaving their bags with reception, but one of those cases is from months back!'

'Oh, you found Lost Property,' Fraser replied, casually inspecting a glass against the light for smears. 'You'd be amazed what people leave behind. I keep it for a while, see if it gets claimed.'

'And if it doesn't?'

'Kerching,' he said with a grin, 'eBay.' Then his face dropped. 'I can't sell the yellow one. That's hers.' He pointed to the far corner, where Krishna saw the same tatty page he'd seen on the noticeboard outside. The missing girl. Her smiling face, fading. Strips of Sellotape were curling away from its corners, repelled by the nicotine veneer on the wall. She looked so happy, Krishna thought, trapped, beaming out of a printed page from the past. It made him shudder. 'Cops have been through it,' Fraser continued, 'but the family won't take it back. They reckon she's still alive. Told me to keep it until she comes back.' After a small stretch of silence Fraser said quietly, 'Can't see it, myself.'

'Wait, really?' Krishna asked. 'She might have just gone into Spain – I mean, that happens, right?

'And left all her stuff?' the Scotsman asked. As he swirled the dregs in his glass he sang a muttered refrain from an old Queen song, 'And another one gone, and another one gone ...'

'You make it sound like people go missing all the time.'

'Not really,' said Fraser. 'Couple in the last year. Like you say, wandered over the border, probably. Half the people on this rock came to get away from something. "Missing" is what they'd rather be.'

'Get away from what?' Krishna asked.

'You name it. Wives. Tax man.'

He pondered a third suggestion for a moment, before Krishna said, 'Overdue library books,' which made Fraser chuckle.

'Seriously, Chris. I've heard it all. And worse. Three golden rules in this bar.' He pointed to three grimy brass monkeys squatting, cemented in filth, on a shelf among dusty bottles. 'See no evil, hear no evil, speak no evil.'

'Suits me, mate,' said Krishna. 'I'm supposed to be in my sickbed. If anyone asks, I wasn't even here.' With a wink drained his glass and bellowed, 'Barman! Another!'

Nine

Petra gasped short gulps of air, fear gripping her chest so tightly that her lungs would allow nothing more. The second man was as different from the first as it was possible to imagine. Short, dumpy, a round, stubbled face shiny with oily sweat, he reminded Petra of a Tunisian market trader. A fez on his head would have completed the stereotype. The eighteen-inch machete glinting in his right hand was less jolly. He kept his distance, eyes flitting into the shadows around them. The lanky Algerian did all the talking, his revolver held so casually it looked like a natural extension of his bony hand. 'Five naughty monkeys.' He shook his head slowly and sucked his teeth, as if their death sentence was a foregone conclusion.

'Dude, we didn't take anything!' said Dane. 'I only opened it!'

'Look, we're from here,' Ed said, his voice a steady authority after Dane's panic. 'You don't need to worry about us. We're actually on our way out. Didn't see a thing.'

The hollow eyes of the tall man bored silently into Ed's. He was completely still, while Ed shifted his weight awkwardly. Then Carly sniffed back tears and blurted, 'We were just looking for my engagement ring! Honest! Please!' at which the gangster gently shushed her like a parent calming a hysterical child. He slammed shut the lid of the cocaine-filled ammo box and placed the paraffin lamp on it, the flickering flame causing his looming shadow to leer high above them, a shifting giant bearing down on its prey. Petra flicked her eyes between him, the darkness which offered no obvious escape route, and the fat machete-man, who skulked a few paces away looking as nervous as she was.

The tall one reached a long arm into the pocket of his baggy combat trousers, slung low on thin hips. Petra saw him pull out a fistful of gold, then return half the haul to his pocket with a clinking of metal. Not gold. Brass. A clutch of bullets. 'Five naughty monkeys,' he repeated, and flipped the revolver chamber from the side of his pistol. As he slid each bullet into its cylinder, he casually pointed the barrel at each one of them. 'Un.' *Shunk,* went the bullet as he looked at Ed. 'Deux.' *Shunk.* Mary shrank away from the barrel. 'Trois.' He smiled at Petra. *Shunk.* She held his gaze. He stopped smiling and turned to Carly. 'Quatre.' *Shunk,* his thumb pushed another .45 calibre into its snug chamber. And as he turned to Dane he pondered the maths for a beat, shrugged and said, 'And two for you.' *Shunk, shunk,* the final death sentence sealed with a slap of the gun, locked and loaded.

'Wait!' Petra heard herself say. 'Just wait.' He looked at her, almost amused. Her friends looked at her, too. 'You don't have to do this. It's … unnecessary.' The tall man looked confused, bordering on pissed off. It was a stupidly long word and she knew it. 'I mean, you don't *need* to. You will *never* see us or hear from us again. *Ever!*'

He shook his head and said to his partner over his shoulder, 'Worst thing about doing deals on this fucking rock. Tourists and monkeys.'

Mary joined Petra's plea, her cheeks stained with grubby tears. 'We're just tour guides. We're lost. We just –'

He chopped the gun towards her and she stopped. The fat Tunisian had made a noise and turned to face the darkness. Something wasn't right. The Algerian turned, keeping his gun raised and targeted. His fat friend took a few steps away and a glimpse of white torchlight cracked the darkness from within. Then Petra heard footsteps.

'The policeman!' whispered Mary.

'HELP!' shouted Petra, and a splintering pain shot through her head as the gun whipped her scalp with effortless accuracy. She fell to her knees, wet rock spinning in front of her. The swooshy sound of her friends' cries morphed into the sound of words. She looked up, pulling focus on the new light. It wasn't a cop. It was two more men, difficult to make out in the shadows, but in the lamplight the one holding the torch looked like the Spanish football coaches Petra had seen on those soccer TV shows her ex, Zach, had watched: glossy hair and baggy sportswear. They stopped in their tracks when they saw the scene before them.

'Que?'

'Esta bien,' said the Tunisian, placing his free hand on the shoulder of the visitor, who backed away.

'Nononono. This is not what we planned.' He raised his arm to shield himself from the five pairs of frightened eyes gazing at him. The other man pulled his T-shirt up to mask his face as they backed into the dark.

'Attendez! Aucun problème!' assured the Tunisian, but this deal had already turned rotten.

'Vamos!' said the Spaniard from the dark, and Petra heard their feet jogging away as the LED light danced away with them and was consumed by blackness.

'Merde!' The Tunisian spun round to face his partner, unsure of what to do. 'Ahmed?'

Their captor looked furious but stayed steely. 'Go after them.' He sighed, raised his gun towards Ed, and while the tubby Tunisian took off after his prey, Petra saw a slender finger slowly pull the trigger, lifting the pistol's hammer.

In a flash she burst into motion – a crash and a blaze of light, as she kicked the paraffin lamp up at Ahmed. It showered him with broken glass and fuel, which immediately burst alight. He reeled back, terrified, his fear resurrected from whatever blaze had scarred his face. He was shaking his arm, the sleeve alight, flames making sweeping patterns in the dark. Dane grabbed Carly and ran, almost through Petra, who spun and followed them with Ed and Mary. The light behind them was fading fast. Petra knew that paraffin burned bright, but not for long, and judging by the angry roar from Ahmed he wasn't about to curl up and die. He'd be right behind them. As they rounded a bend a shot rang out and she heard the bullet ricochet off a couple of walls, along with Carly's scream.

They ran. Harder. Further. Arms outstretched, effectively blind, until eventually Ed panted, 'Wait!' and they slowed to a halt. Mary switched on her torch but Ed slapped his hand over it. In the eerie red light through his flesh, he held his finger to his lips, then cupped his hand to his ear and they all understood. Silence. They listened. No shooting. No shouting. Nothing. After what felt like an age, Mary spoke.

'Is everyone OK?'

'Yeah, I'm OK,' said Petra.

'Are you fucking kidding?' sniffed Carly, wiping her nose on her arm. 'OK?!'

'Come on, let's get out of here,' Ed said, resuming command and leading them further into the gloom.

'Which way *is* out?' Mary asked.

'Noooooooo!' wailed Carly, which got shushes from the others.

'Seriously, Ed,' said Dane. 'Where the fuck are we?' But Ed shushed him too. After only a few seconds they stopped at a corner where two tunnels met. Ed held up his hand to halt them. They heard distant voices echoing down the tunnels, shouting but muffled, unclear. Carly was fighting the urge to sob, her chest shaking while Dane clasped his arm around her stooped shoulders.

Then Petra had an idea. She pulled her phone from her pocket and checked the screen. 'No signal, obviously. But if we could get to an outside wall?'

One of the echoing shouts sounded closer and Carly whispered through snotty tears, 'They're gonna kill us.'

'I've had enough of this,' growled Dane, and grabbing Carly's hand he barged past Ed and Mary and pulled her with him down the tunnel that seemed quietest.

'Wait!' Mary shouted in a hoarse whisper.

Petra was gripped by momentary indecision. She didn't fancy either of the choices ahead, but faced with going back the way they'd come or getting separated, she dragged herself into motion and followed. Ed did the same, Mary reluctantly still calling after them, 'Wait!'

Ten

'Wait, wait!' shouted Krishna above the laughter. 'You're telling me that I could *swim* to Africa!' He was holding court, well lubricated and enjoying the company. A few of the locals had joined him at the bar.

Fraser cast an obvious look up and down Krishna's portly physique and replied, 'Well, maybe not *you,*' which got a laugh from his audience. 'But aye, it's only twelve miles across the water, to an entirely different continent. This place has been a smugglers' paradise for centuries. Still is. Get yourself an inflatable with a decent outboard and a few dodgy contacts – you're in business.'

'God, I wish my mate Dane could hear all this.'

'Into all that is he? Dodgy dealing?'

'No, no. He's just a fitness freak. And a show-off. If you bet him he couldn't swim it he'd be standing here in his Speedos before you could say "Mine's a pint."'

'Mine's a pint,' one of the locals said.

'I walked into that.' Krishna pushed their empty glasses across the bar. 'Same again, squire.'

'Where are they?' asked Fraser, refilling the empties. 'Your mates?'

'They're inside the bloody Rock. *Again.* His girlfriend dropped her engagement ring in there so they've gone looking for it.'

'Now?' asked Fraser, checking his watch. Krishna saw him exchange a worried glance with the man waiting for his beer, and felt the mood darken. The locals examined their drinks, or their shoes.

He looked at the pair, waiting for an explanation. 'What?'

PETRA HAD COME on this holiday unable to trust a man. Now, lost and confused, she felt exactly the same way about Carly's boyfriend. And Ed, for that matter. She was coming to the conclusion that they were both testosterone-fuelled idiots, full of bravado and bullshit.

'Dane!' she called. 'Stop! Where are we going?'

He slowed a little as the torch on his phone showed a dark opening in the side of the damp, shimmering wall: another path off to the right, another choice in a maze of confusing indecision. The group collected in a bunch, their only sound the shallow panting of misty breath. Eventually Mary said, 'I think they've gone,' but her wide eyes scanning the black space behind them told Petra she didn't really believe it.

'Come on,' said Dane moving forwards. 'This way.'

'Wait, no hang on.' Ed was peering into the second tunnel. 'It feels like we need to head right. The outside is this way, isn't it?'

Petra didn't have any faith in either of them, but made her decision. 'You're right. Dane, wait!' But before there was any debate Dane pulled Carly ahead, ignoring Petra. With a shrug, Ed followed Carly, so inevitably Mary followed him. Petra swore and found herself once again trailing at the back of the line as they trod carefully around a bend and past another hollowed-out blast-trap like the one Ed had explained, a lifetime ago.

The straggle of friends became more bunched up as Dane's lead slowed. The passage, more rough and jagged than the others, was getting narrower. Petra noticed that the roof was getting lower, too, tiny stalactites getting closer as they walked, and soon Dane was having to walk with a stoop. Suddenly a noise behind her made Petra jump. They had all heard it, and stopped, peering back into blackness.

Carly was the first to whisper what they were all thinking. 'What was that?'

Ed quietly hissed 'Shhh', and their shallow breathing was all Petra could hear. Then it happened again. Tap, tap, tap, like something hard knocking against the rock.

'What the hell?' whispered Mary to Ed, who just repeated: 'Shhh ...'

Silence filled the tunnel for the next few seconds until the tapping sound became a rattle, then a scrape. It was getting closer. Petra heard Carly whimper and saw her clamp herself around Dane's solid waist. He responded by taking decisive action. 'Let's get out of here.' He pushed forward into the tight tunnel, quicker than before, almost at a jog, his head bowed to avoid the spiky roof. In the swinging beam of her torch, Petra saw him disappear from view as the tunnel turned to the left, and then she heard a yelp from Carly and ran around the bend to find … a wall.

Dane had his hands pressed up against the dead end. 'What?' He couldn't make sense of it. 'What the … Why …?' Ed and Mary started doing the same as Petra, scanning their torches around the tunnel walls, looking for any glimmer of hope. They were surrounded by solid rock. The tunnel simply stopped.

'Unfinished,' murmured Ed.

'Un … finished?' repeated Carly, unable to believe him.

Dane attempted to stay calm, sweeping his phone torch across the black walls. 'Don't worry, babe, there'll be a –' but his reassuring words were cut short by a clatter behind them. They all spun round, training their torch beams at the curved wall of the passage, but seeing nothing. A rattle. Another tap. Clear as a bell, closer than before.

'We're gonna have to go back,' stated Petra.

Carly emitted a whining, 'Noooooo,' which was squished into muffled silence by Dane's palm over her mouth.

'Shh, babe.'

Ed whispered a command. 'Cut the torches. Sound travels down here. He might not be in *this* tunnel.'

'No point advertising that we're here,' Petra agreed, and all three torches clicked off.

'Shit. This is killing my battery,' Dane murmured, cutting the torch on his phone.

Blackness engulfed them, shoulder to shoulder, crammed tight into the deadly tunnel that had tricked them. Nowhere to run.

Silence but for clammy puffs of breath. Then, from nowhere, *whoosh!* A glowing green rush of light hit them. Literally, a plastic tube of light hit Ed in the face. He swore and the glow-stick bounced to his feet. As one, they all looked from the glowing green stick on the ground back up into the tunnel, but saw nothing.

Carly squeaked, 'Who's there?' but the only response was the echo of *tap, tap, tap* on the rock.

Petra quietly asked, 'Are they fucking with us?'

'We're trapped,' wept Carly. 'We're dead.'

'Not yet,' replied Ed. 'Just wait.' He took a couple of paces forward into the darkness towards the noise.

Mary hissed, 'Edward! No!'

He turned and spat a whispered reply. 'Mary! Please!'

She gripped his hand. 'I won't lose you! I can't!'

'Listen to me. I won't let us die down here.' He looked out into the dark. 'I am *not* going out like this.'

He picked up the glow-stick and threw it back along the tunnel, casting eerie light on damp, black walls as it rattled to a stop. He was squinting, they all were, desperate to see the approaching threat. The dark mouth of the disappearing space within the green walls looked like the entrance to a monster's lair. Suddenly, with a clatter and scrape, the glow-stick gained impossible life and skittered back towards them.

Dane swore under his breath and Petra said, 'How?'

'Torch!' instructed Ed, and Petra lit the way for him. He was only eight or nine paces from the glow-stick but they held their breath as he slowly limped towards it. Mary trod carefully after him whispering, 'Please be careful,' her own torch finding nothing but empty space.

Petra followed, a feeling of dread in her stomach, a musky smell of damp filling her nostrils. Suddenly she gasped. 'Did you see that?'

'What?' asked Ed.

She was sure she'd seen movement, a glimpse of something moving fast through the darkness. 'Up ahead!' she pointed her torch into the bend of the tunnel but found nothing. Ed kept walking towards the glow-stick lying dormant on the ground. Just a couple of paces away he was halted by a rapidly approaching sound – patter, tap, scrape, coming at them fast. Before he could retreat it was on them.

A rock ape snatched the glow-stick up and bared its teeth at Ed. He visibly relaxed, and Petra felt all the air leave her chest. Dane said, 'Oh you've got to be kidding me,' and Petra saw what had been making the eerie scraping, tapping noises: in its other hand the ape held the tattered remains of Krishna's selfie-stick. It spun on its haunches and took off back down the tunnel away from them, a bobbing green glow floating away with the familiar tap, tap, scrape of the broken selfie-stick.

'Oh my God,' panted Carly.

'Curious little buggers, aren't they?' said Petra.

'Was that –?' started Mary.

'Krishna's selfie-stick,' answered Dane.

'How the hell did he activate that glow-stick?'

asked Mary.

'Bent it?' replied Ed.

'Or bit it,' added Petra.

Dane was shaking his head in disbelief, and said, 'What a bastard,' under his breath. Carly wiped tears from her cheek and gripped Dane tightly around his waist.

'Come on, hun,' he reassured. 'We're gonna be all right.'

Ed walked onwards to the kink in the tunnel, checked around the corner and beckoned the others to join him. 'All clear. Let's go back and then head the other way. Agreed?'

Petra nodded. Dane continued trying to calm Carly. 'See? We'll be fine. It was just a stupid monkey. We hit a dead end, but that's rare – right, Ed?'

'Right.'

'We'll be out of here in no time. And we're OK, aren't we, hun? We've got each other. We've got three really good torches.' As if on cue, Mary's torch blinked on and off. She hit it with the palm of her hand and it flickered, then died. A couple more strikes of her hand did nothing to revive it. 'We've got two really good torches.'

Carly sniffled and pulled a pink, slender phone

from her pocket, swiped the screen to light the teeny white torchlight and immediately looked defeated. 'Battery's nearly dead,' she croaked.

'We should save our phones,' Petra instructed. 'Here, use this.' She took a glow-stick from her back pocket, cracked it and handed it to Carly, the green glow illuminating her mascara-streaked cheeks. She looked monstrous, but smiled weakly as she put her phone away. They gathered at the bend behind Ed, who once again assumed the tone of a military leader. 'With me. I'll lead.'

He stepped forward just a pace, extending his own grey plastic glow-stick ahead of him before reaching forward to crack its contents into vibrant chemical life. Sweeping the luminous green tube ahead of him, there was nothing but empty space. He glanced back at the group and beckoned them to follow. The moment they did, he turned and yelped.

The grotesque scarred face of Ahmed, the Algerian gangster, loomed into the green light from his blast-trap hiding place. He grinned and said, 'Boo.'

Petra screamed, and that's all she heard: shouting, yells of terror and the scrabbling of feet on slippy rock. She saw the gangster raise his gun before a well-aimed *swish* from Dane's boot slammed into the Algerian's forearm, sending the gun spinning off into the dark. Ed launched himself at the wiry villain and toppled him to the ground, giving Petra an open path before her. Instinctively she grabbed Carly and ran past the grappling mass of Ed, Ahmed and now Dane fighting on the damp floor. Mary followed them, screaming for Ed to come, too. Petra saw Dane slam Ahmed's head against the ground and he shouted, 'Come on!' springing to his feet.

Ed hauled himself up to follow but screamed in pain. Petra spun around to see Ahmed, strewn across the floor, wet with blood, grabbing Ed's foot. Ed twisted like a snared rabbit and, to her horror, Petra watched his lower leg wrench free. Carly screamed and for a second the puzzled Algerian looked baffled to be holding an alloy prosthetic limb, which he quickly dropped in disgust. Ed slumped forwards into Mary's arms and Dane flew back at Ahmed to finish the job.

A kick to the gangster's ribs threw Dane off balance and he slipped down onto one knee. Petra didn't see what happened but in an instant Dane was on his back and the tenacious gangster, glistening with blood and sweat, was overpowering him with an onslaught of punches. Petra's attention was on something else, something on the ground. She stooped, grappled, ran at the pair, and, with a batter's swing and an almighty metallic *clang,* slammed the prosthetic into the side of Ahmed's head. A spray of blood, black in the green glow, splattered Dane's face. The thin, muscular gangster slid sideways, unconscious, his shoulders awkwardly propped against the wall of the narrow tunnel.

Panting and ferocious, Petra raised the weapon for a second swing, but Dane stopped her.

'Woah, woah,' he was saying, getting to his feet. 'Petra, Petra. It's OK.'

Through a veil of red mist, she slowly came to her senses, hearing Dane's voice as if through deep water.

'Petra?' he was repeating. She was staring at the catatonic body slumped between them. She felt Dane's hand on her shoulder and suddenly snapped back from her trance into reality. Dane was looking at her, cautious, wary, and gently took the blood-smeared alloy leg from her hand.

She felt herself relax. 'Shit. I just –'

But before she could finish the thought, a deafening *CRACK* rang out and the gangster's head exploded before them. Gasping for air, she lurched back and saw that the unscarred half of Ahmed's face had been blown away, leaving the burnt, bloody, sodden mess of half a head lolling on his shoulders.

Carly was screaming. Mary was holding the pistol.

'WHAT THE FUCK?' Dane shouted.

Petra stammered, 'He… he was still breathing! Why did you –?'

'It was self-defence!' blurted Mary with a slight tremor. 'He was going to kill us! Ed? It was self-defence!'

Ed was sitting on the floor, a flat, loose trouser leg flopping below the knee. 'Of course it was. You had no choice.'

Petra felt sick but chose not to argue with a cold woman holding a warm gun. Mary ushered herself past her, crouched at the corpse and used Ahmed's T-shirt to wipe the gun before wrapping the weapon in the dead man's palm.

Dane realised he was holding Ed's prosthetic leg. 'So,' he said, holding it out towards him, 'this is yours.'

Eleven

A world away, a mile through rock and down the hill, in the Luna Rossa bar Krishna was incredulous. 'You're having a laugh, right? It can't be *that* bad. Scary stories to keep the kids away, I reckon.'

Behind the bar Fraser shook his head. Krishna wasn't buying their sinister stories of dangers in the dark within the labyrinthine rock. 'Well,' droned the barman, 'maybe it's not *that* bad. You do hear tales, o' course. Drug dealers, smugglers, but …' he pointed to the nicotine-coated monkeys, sticky with grime, on the shelf. 'I wouldn't know, now, would I?'

Krishna sensed he was playing it down, but the

thought of his friends scouting around in the gloom up there unsettled him. 'I feel a bit bad for Petra. I mean, she had nothing to do with it. Got talked into it, know what I mean?'

'How so?'

'Just, it was bloody Dane who caused Mary to drop Carly's stupid ring in the first place, shoving me into the monkeys.'

'Oh, right,' nodded Fraser. 'So you startled a rock ape?'

'Not me! Well, yes, me, but …' he shook his head. 'I'm sure it won't take long to find,' he said, trying to convince himself. 'I mean, they know where Mary dropped it.'

'Aye,' agreed Fraser. 'You wait, they'll be walking though that door any minute, diamond on her finger, drinks all round. No need for you to worry.'

'The monkeys alone are enough to stop me going back,' he muttered. 'Ahh, they'll be fine,' he decided, and took a swig of his pint.

'IS IT GOING TO WORK?' asked Mary. She was crouching next to Ed, who was grappling to reattach his bent and bloody prosthetic leg to a smooth stump of flesh just below his knee. Petra had never seen a prosthesis being attached. Its moulded cup and straps were fascinating, but at the same time it felt rude to stare.

'It'll do,' grunted Ed. 'But they're not really built for bludgeoning.'

Petra instinctively apologised, which sounded silly given that she'd just saved their lives. Ed pushed himself up against the wall and stood on his feet. The boot on the fake foot jutted inwards at an odd angle but a few tentative steps with Mary at his side revealed he could walk on it.

'How did it happen?' asked Carly. 'The leg.'

'Occupational hazard.'

'Iraq or Afghanistan?' asked Dane.

'Come on, we've got to get out,' Mary interrupted. 'The other guys could still be in here somewhere.'

'Hang on,' Petra said. 'What about him?'

They looked at her, waiting for more.

'Well, we can't just leave him, can we?'

'It's not a "him", it's a cadaver,' Mary corrected. 'Just tissue and bones.'

This woman had the ability to make Petra's hackles rise every time she opened her mouth.

'That's not the point, Mary, I just don't think it's right to –'

But before she could continue Ed put his hand on her shoulder and said, 'Petra, it's OK. We'll tell the police what happened when we get out. They'll deal with it. You won't be in any trouble.'

'I won't be in any trouble? What the fuck is that supposed to mean?' But he'd turned away and Mary was trotting after him. She looked to Carly for support but Dane was pulling her in Mary's wake. She followed them, anger, regret and guilt twisting at her insides. After a few moments she cast a glance back down the tunnel and saw darkness swallowing the coagulating corpse. In a few steps it had vanished. Her violence erased from view.

After a minute or so of stifling silence they moved past a tunnel opening that appeared to go uphill and Carly held Dane back. 'Wait,' she said. 'This one looks like it goes up. Shouldn't we go up?'

'Er ... I thought we were going with Ed,' Petra replied. 'We've literally *just* agreed that.' She was still pissed off and her tone sounded condescending, but Carly didn't seem to notice.

Carly turned to Ed. 'But you said the tunnels

further up were easier. The concert hall, remember? I'm going up.'

But Dane held her back. 'Wait.'

'We should head towards the edge,' advised Ed. 'We're bound to hit an outer wall eventually.'

Petra nodded, which seemed to annoy Carly, who turned on Ed.

'Who the fuck put you in charge? You're as lost as we are! Come on, Dane. Let's head for the top.' But Dane didn't follow her. He stood fast. In the dim torchlight and green hue of a glow-stick Petra saw frustration on his face: to stay with the group or leave with his hot-headed fiancé …?

'Ed?' he asked. 'Shouldn't we go up?'

'Going up means going back in. We should stick together and head for the edge.'

Carly shook her head in disbelief at Dane's lack of loyalty. She squared up to Ed and Mary. 'We trusted you guys. We trusted you because you said you knew this place and *now* look at us! We're totally fucking lost! There are men with guns who want to kill us! And –' she thrust her hand back towards the dead end '– we've murdered someone! Correction. *You* murdered someone. Both of you.' She pointed at Petra. 'I'm getting the fuck out of here.'

Heat rose up Petra's neck. 'Fuck you!' It

stopped Carly short. 'Just fuck you, Carly. We're only *in* this place because of you!'

Then Mary joined her. 'That's right. I haven't heard you say thanks, or sorry. Thanks for helping me look for my shitty ring. Thanks for saving my shitty life. Sorry for nearly getting you all slaughtered.'

'Back the fuck off!' Petra jabbed a finger at Mary. She didn't need her as an ally. 'None of this would have happened if it weren't for you!'

'It was Carly who begged to come down here!'

'WELL, I'M NOT THE ONE WHO DROPPED THE FUCKING RING!' Carly yelled. The three of them were nose to nose, bellowing spittle at each other. Ed pulled Mary away. 'This isn't getting us anywhere.'

Mary took a few breaths, calmed herself and resumed a schoolmistress-like tone. 'You're right, darling. Of course. Carly, I'm sorry about your ring, but really, you don't know what you're talking about. It's a maze up there. Come with us.'

Carly spat back, 'If anyone here is clueless, love, it's you. I'm going up. Up, and out. Come on, Dane.' Dane looked torn. He looked to Petra but she had nothing to say. That moment of hesitation was all it took. Carly flung his hand from her grip and through choked tears said, 'I can't fucking believe you,' before stomping away into the darkness of the rising passage.

'Carly!' Dane called, but she kept on walking. He sighed and turned back to the group. 'Shit, sorry guys. I'll go get her.' He started up the slope but Ed grabbed his elbow to stop him.

'Wait, Dane. It's a labyrinth in there. The last thing we need is *two* of you getting lost. You stay with us. Mary, you go and fetch Carly because you know the upper tunnels better than anyone. We'll wait for you at the barracks room. It's just down here. Remember?' She nodded. 'It's safe if we just sit tight till you're both back with us.'

She walked up the passage with one of the two remaining torches and Petra felt the darkness push in around them.

THE LUNA ROSSA was quieter now. The TV had been muted and most of the regulars had gone home. In an almost empty room one man was full. Full of beer, full of warmth and full of slightly slurred technical information. 'It's an HDR lenzz, 5G, UHR screen – that's Ulchra-High Rezlooshun.'

Krishna was proudly displaying his new gadget to a patient audience of one. 'Look,' he beckoned, swiping photographs across the glossy screen. ''Mazin' quality for a phone.'

Fraser leaned forward, squinting at the brightly coloured photograph of Krishna's gang of friends standing in the sunshine up on the rock earlier, a palm-sized slice of happy lives. He lifted the phone from Krishna's hand and curled his lip.

'What?' asked Krishna.

Fraser snorted indifference and rolled his eyes. 'Edward Pilkington,' he muttered.

'Who? The military guy? He's up there with them now. You know him?'

Fraser handed the phone back and said, 'Oh, aye. This is Gib, remember. Everybody knows *everybody*. He's not military, sunshine. Call of bloody Duty on the X-Box; that's all the military experience Ed the cripple's had.'

Krishna felt a wince of discomfort at Andy's archaic language. 'What d'you mean, erm … cripple?'

Fraser dug his thumbs into the arch of his lower back and Krishna heard a crack. The barman breathed a satisfied sigh and said, 'He's got a false leg. Had some sorta blood disease when he was a kid. Had a prosthesis since he was a wee lad. Hop-along *wishes* he'd been in the army,' said the Scotsman. 'Wanted to be an army medic. Till he dropped out of medical college. Not many places in Her Majesty's armed forces for one-legged quitters. We're not *that* near the bottom of the barrel yet, thank Christ.'

Krishna was confused by this new information. He was certain Ed had said he was in the army. But before his fuddled brain could replay their earlier meeting, Fraser was pointing to the photo and asking him a question. 'So these two are a couple. They're in room three. And this girl? Are you and her together?'

'What, Petra? Naaaa. I reckon that was their plan. Dane's my mate from work, and his girlfriend Carly – sorry, *fiancé* – is trying to set me up with her. They go back years, I think.'

'Well, that's clearly going very well,' Fraser drawled, 'given that you're sitting on yer arse down here.'

'Hmmm. I kinda messed things up when I got spooked by that bloody monkey. Made a right tit of myself.'

This drew a good rasping laugh from Fraser. 'Behold! The fearless red-blooded Englishman! In

114

the quest for the maiden's hand, nothing can defeat him! Except a monkey.' This reduced him to coughing fits of mirth.

'Yeah, yeah, whatever,' said Krishna. 'You weren't there. Anyway, you're too scared to go up there in the dark! You just said as much!'

'True,' agreed Fraser. 'But so are you.'

'What? I'd go up there right now.'

The barman raised an eyebrow and said, 'Away then, mighty warrior.'

'Y'know what?' said Krishna, draining his pint and slamming the glass on the bar. 'I bloody will. I'm gonna walk back up there, give 'em a call and see where they are. I'm back in the band!'

'That's the spirit, wee man,' laughed Fraser. 'Amazing what some Dutch courage can do. Go get her.'

Krishna stood up. 'Sir, it's been a pleasure. I shall return, the conquering hero, with a beautiful maiden upon my arm.'

'Or failing that,' added Fraser, 'that Petra lass.' He chortled at his own joke then held up a scrap of paper with some scribbled numbers on it. 'Shall I put these on sir's room?'

With a nod Krishna was out the door, the fresh night air on his face and a mission on his mind.

PETRA HAD NEVER seen anything like this. She was standing in a long, professionally dug military barrack area. It had bench seats cut into the rock and further up the walls her sweeping torch found cut-outs, shelves and bunk space. 'How did we walk past this? I don't remember seeing –'

She was interrupted by Dane. 'What the hell am I doing? What am I doing just standing here? I should have gone after her.'

'Dane, relax,' instructed Ed. 'Stop pacing. Sit. Mary will find her.'

'How can you just sit there? I should be doing something. Why did I let her go?'

'Mary will find her,' Ed repeated, sounding bored.

'How do you know?'

'No one knows these tunnels as well as Mary.'

Dane laughed a hopeless guffaw. 'Yeah, right! Then why are we lost, Ed?'

'Because of you.'

Dane stopped walking a groove into the centre of the room. 'How the fuck d'you work that out?'

Ed was calm in his response. 'You barged ahead

when Mary was telling you to wait.'

'What?'

'You remember,' he smiled, 'back when I had two working legs and Petra hadn't bludgeoned a man to death.'

'Woah,' said Petra. 'He was still breathing! It was your psychotic girlfriend who –'

But Ed spoke over her, the belligerent army general returning to the surface. 'You barged ahead when Mary was telling you to wait. We had no choice but to follow you.'

'Well you're the fucking tour guide!' shouted Dane.

'And you're the idiot who got us trapped down a dead end,' Ed spat through gritted teeth.

'Just shut up! Both of you!' Petra was holding her hand in the air, like a child in class wanting to speak. They both looked at her. She turned to face the high wall and slowly scanned her dim torch beam across its ridges and ledges. 'I've got an idea.'

WITH THE LIGHTS OF the town behind him, Krishna strode purposefully away from the yellow warmth of the Luna Rossa towards the dark, pointed shadow towering up from the ground before him. Every step towards the menacing silhouette sapped his beer-fuelled bravado just a little, and by the time he reached the foot of the long, winding path up the rock, the thought of the warm bed he'd left behind had a magnetic pull on his unfit body.

'C'mon, man,' he whispered to himself. 'You've got this.' He surveyed the ground in the moonlight. The path banked gently off to his right but looking up he could see the main entrance they had stood at a few hours ago. There was a much shorter route if he climbed up the grassy, gravelly slope. There were shrubs, and he knew how big some of the spiders were in those shrubs, but he calculated a course that would avoid those. He tried dialling Dane's phone again, but again, as in the previous four attempts, it went straight to voicemail. He looked back at the shimmering lights of Gibraltar town, then up the steep bank to the mouth of the monstrous rock. They think I'm tucked up with a dicky tummy watching Netflix, he thought. And I could be. If I turn around I could be back in my room in fifteen minutes.

But he saw Fraser's mocking grin as he walked

back in, alone, defeated. A coward, scared by his own shadow. He looked up at the Goliath of a rock. He could regain some lost pride, possibly regain some lost ground with Petra. The fire in his belly reignited.

'OK, buddy. Let's do this,' he said aloud. 'Climb the hill, meet the others, get the ring. Easy.' He cracked his knuckles and started heaving his weight up the steep bank, around shrubs, across shale, a more or less straight line up. 'Climb the hill, meet the others, get the ring,' he repeated like a mantra. 'I sound like bloody Frodo.'

'HELP ME UP.' Petra handed the torch to Ed.

'What?'

'Not you, Ed. No offence, but … Dane, give me a leg up.'

'Why?' asked Ed.

She was pulling Dane towards the wall, positioning him in a particular spot. She offered him her foot and he dutifully cupped his hands beneath it. She pushed herself up, pulled her phone from her back pocket and with an athletic twist stepped up onto a high, chiselled-out shelf.

'Higher up,' she explained, 'I might get a signal.'

Dane tutted like his effort had been for nothing. 'You reckon?'

She had her stomach flat to the wall, her feet spaced wide on the shelf and the side of her forehead was touching cold, damp rock where it arced across to the ceiling above her. Moving slowly, she lifted her phone in an outstretched hand.

Ed said, 'Careful, Petra,' and Dane stood below her, braced to catch.

She raised it high and pressed the screen. It illuminated to reveal no signal strength at all. Also, the battery indicator was red and showing five per cent.

'Anything?' asked Dane.

'About to die,' she grunted, reaching as high as she could without toppling backwards. With a gasp, she gave up. 'My phone's crap. I've got nothing. Pass me yours.' She tossed her phone down to Dane, who grumbled, 'This is pointless,' as he passed his own phone up to her. She returned to her tall stretch and almost lost her balance when she saw the screen light up. 'One bar!'

'No way!' said Dane.

'Really?' asked Ed.

She tentatively manoeuvred her thumb across the screen, as if the lone bar of signal strength might be frightened by sudden movements and flit away into the ether. 'Nine, nine, nine,' she said, tapping the screen. The phone started to dial and she heard a tiny voice. 'Hello! Hello!' she yelled and tapped the speaker icon. The tinny voice resonated more clearly: '… number you have dialled is not valid. Please check the number and re-dial.'

'Shit,' said Dane. 'Try again.'

She hung up and even more slowly started to redial, muttering, 'Nine, nine –' but before she could finish the phone burst into life playing an upbeat pop hit by Pharrel Williams. The words 'Big Krish' lit the screen. 'It's Krishna!' she yelped, and tapped the green button.

'Krish!' shouted Dane.

'Dane? Hello?' Krishna's voice was loud and made Petra laugh with relief.

'Oh, thank God,' smiled Dane, and Petra said, 'Krishna, it's Petra. Get help! We're lost in here!'

Out on the hillside Krishna stopped in his tracks, panting, clasping his phone to his ear. 'What? Wait. Where are you? Did you find the ring?' He heard Petra's voice say something about lower tunnels and a side entrance but it crackled and bits were missing. 'Say that again!' he said. 'I'm losing you.'

In the barrack cave she shouted again. 'We're in the lower tunnels! We came through a side entrance! There are men ...' Then the three of them heard the crackle and pop of Krishna's voice saying, 'Right ... What?' Petra repeated herself and added, 'We can't find Carly.'

Krishna put his hand over his other ear and heard a man's voice – Dane, he guessed – saying something about barracks. 'OK, OK, stay put!' he shouted. 'I can see a police car near the tunnel. I'm bringing help.'

The three prisoners were craning their necks, desperate to hear their rescuer's plan, but the phone crackled, then beeped. The call had been dropped.

'Has he gone?' asked Ed.

'Lost the signal,' reported Petra.

'Well, it sounds like help is on the way. Thank God for your friend.'

Twelve

This is it, thought Krishna. This is bloody well *it!*

Finally, after years of being the hopeless hanger-on, the fifth wheel, the also-ran, *this* was his time to shine. He would fetch help, find his friends and be the hero of a story they would tell until their dying day.

Spurred on by the scent of glory, with Petra's pleas for help ringing in his ears, he scrambled up the steep slope to the level ground near the mouth of the Rock's main tunnel. Panting, scratched and filthy, he staggered across to the squad car, peered in at the driver's window and found it empty. His heart sank. As quickly as that his wondrous fantasy of heroism was dribbling away, like rain through his crappy trainers. He looked around but he was alone. 'Hello?' he said into the gloom.

A few metres inside the mouth of the tunnel was the gate he'd watched Ed lock up at the end of their tour. He stood at the bars looking into the black hole beyond. 'Hello? Anyone?' He thought he heard a noise from within and lit the torch on his phone, but its tiny light was swallowed whole in the endless cavern. He stood silent for a few moments but heard nothing.

Recalling the half-heard snatch of what Petra had said, he started scouting for a side entrance and quickly found the path his friends had used earlier. At the old iron gate he gave it a shove and it scraped open with a grinding moan. With none of the gentle caution his mates had demonstrated, he stomped through the litter, oblivious to the ape-corpse, ducked under the low ridge and into the inner tunnel, shouting their names.

'Dane! Petra!'

It was so dark, even the light from his phone-torch only served to illuminate black walls surrounding yet more black, empty space. After a few strong paces forwards, he slipped. The ground to his right dropped away and in a blink he was on his side, sliding out of control. With his phone still clamped in his hand, his flailing arms failed to find anything to arrest his descent. A flimsy plastic fence escaped his flapping grasp and scratched his back as he skimmed beneath it. Slippy rock got steeper and faster … then vanished. He screamed for the second that he was in space, without rock, without light, without any sense of up from down, falling helpless into death's abyss.

A colossal *SPLASH* took his breath away and he was instantly consumed by icy, black water.

A STRANGE NOISE, an echo of a distant slap reverberating from the belly of the Rock made Petra, Dane and Ed stop talking. Petra felt her ears prick at a nearer sound, a scuff outside the barrack cave, and then Mary appeared in the dark. Ed swung the torchlight onto her. She was breathless, dishevelled, had a scratch on her face. She also appeared to have lost her torch.

'Where's Carly?' asked Dane.

'I was about to ask you the same thing,' she replied. 'I thought she'd come back.'

Petra swore, and Ed asked, 'What happened to you?'

Mary wiped her face with her forearm. 'It was the smugglers. Had to run. Don't worry, they didn't see me.'

'How can you be sure?' asked Dane.

'They might have followed you back!' Petra said, her sinews suddenly alive with fight-or-flight energy.

'We should go,' commanded Ed.

But Petra fought the urge to flee. 'No, wait. Hang on. Krishna's getting the police. We should stay here. We told him where we were. He said stay put.'

'You spoke to Krishna?' asked Mary.

'You're wrong, Petra,' said Ed. 'We need to keep moving.'

'Ed's right,' agreed his ragged partner. 'They could still be following me. We should go.'

'We need to find Carly!' Dane bellowed.

'I heard the smugglers back up there,' Mary continued, moving towards the entrance with Ed. 'We should head this way.'

'I'm not going any further without Carly. I'm not walking away from her.'

THE CRYSTAL LAKE had slept undisturbed deep in the heart of the Rock of Gibraltar for decades. In all its millennia of silent formation it had never had such a rude awakening. Flapping, gasping, coughing and retching, Krishna clawed his way through freezing darkness until his feet found firm ground at the water's edge. Firm, but slippy. He was on his belly, elbow-crawling out of the icy pond, panting, his shocked heart racing. After a few seconds of resting flat out on the cold rock, enough time for him to comprehend what had happened, to realise that he was not dead, he hauled his soaking legs from the water, turned over and found he could sit up.

He blinked drips of water from his eyes and peered into ... nothing. It was utterly black. He'd never experienced complete blindness like this. He knew his eyes were open and yet they may as well have been empty sockets. He turned his head, sure he would see a shimmer, a glint, *anything* that would feed his optic nerve a crumb of information; but the blackness was complete.

He huddled, shivering, terrified. From nowhere,

his stomach cramped and he vomited a bellyful of beer. He was in shock, shuddering, crying.

After a few minutes the only sound was his own shallow breathing, which gradually slowed to normal. He felt cramp in his fingers and realised he was still gripping his phone.

He lifted it, unable to see his own hand in front of his face, shook away the water and pressed its screen. To his complete amazement, it worked. Its 'waterproof' claim had been more than hollow sales patter. 'Huh. Unbreakable,' he muttered to himself. Predictably, it showed that he was without a phone signal, but the glow from its screen immediately lit the space around him: wet rock beneath him, to his left and right, even a foot or so above him. He pressed his thumb on the screen but the lock-screen didn't move. 'Oh. Not unbreakable.' He could live without fingerprint recognition. He rebooted it and entered the eight-figure unlock code. 'Fixed,' he smiled, then swiped to activate the torch, but nothing happened. He repeatedly tapped the torch icon, to no avail. 'Broken,' he admitted.

Then he had an idea. He selected the camera and pointed the phone ahead of him. The screen was predictably black, the lens on the phone pointing into the same dark space that had rendered his own eyes blind. But when he swiped through the options, past *Video, Square, Pano* and a few others, he saw it. *Night.*

Immediately, the screen showed a ghostly green image of the lake before him. 'Woah,' he murmured, impressed by the camera's ability to pick out such detail in utter darkness. He gasped as he panned the camera around to see the size of the cavern he was in. Green ripples on black water stretched away. He couldn't see where they met another wall. This pool was huge.

And now a new fear gripped him. He spun the camera around. He saw the hole above, a black space through which he'd plummeted, way up high in the cavern's roof. He saw stalactites dangle in a million shapes and sizes, green and black fingers pointing down at the cavern's newest victim. He felt small. He felt lost. He felt completely fucked.

There was no way back. The water stretched to God knows where, the walls rose high and slippy on either side. He was on the only bit of rock he could see that was above the water – alive but doomed to die without help.

'DANE!' he yelled. 'CARLY! PETRAAA!'

He listened until the last of his echoing cries dissipated into silence. An occasional drip was the only reply.

He pulled himself onto his knees, turned away from the lake and started feeling the wall with his hand. As he reached up above head height, his hand disappeared into empty space. He yelped and yanked it back in surprise. He pointed his phone camera above him and saw, in the grainy green image, a black hole in the wall. He stood, a squatting crouch all that the low rock above him would allow, and pointed the phone into the hole. Carefully he reached in, dreading what his hand might touch. Monkeys, bats, killer spiders, his imagination was conjuring all these and more.

At full stretch he let out a sigh and finally breathed again. His hand met nothing but air. This moment of relief only compounded a greater dilemma for him to overcome: he'd found a tunnel. A tight one, but big enough to crawl along. He looked back at the lake again. Then back down the black tunnel. He hated them both. He was no swimmer, and yet there was nothing he'd rather do less than squeeze down a dark tunnel into unknown horrors.

He slumped back to his knees and soon found

himself weeping. This was utterly hopeless. His stupid attempt at heroics had got him completely stuck, and now he was faced with impossible choices: swim to his death, crawl to his death, or sit still and starve to death. Not even his state-of-the-art phone could save him now.

Unless … His shoulders stopped their sobbing shudders and he wiped his sniffly nose with the back of his arm. He tapped his phone. Again it requested the unlock code. This was going to get tiresome. He growled, went straight into 'Settings' and disabled the security locks. He was beyond worrying about being hacked. Swipe, swipe, swipe, so many pages of apps, every one entirely useless to him now. Apart from one. Swipe, swipe – there! He tapped an image of a black pool ball bearing a number 8: the Magic Eight Ball app, which he and Dane had once used it to dictate an entire pub crawl.

'Please work,' he said, shaking the phone. Slowly the yellow words floated into view from inside the black ball: 'Don't count on it.'

'Fair enough.' He shook the phone again and said, 'Should I go down the tunnel?' Holding it flat in his palm, he saw it reveal its answer: 'Ask again later.'

'Hmmm. Should I swim for it?' Shake, shake, and the words were again replaced: 'My sources say no.'

'I like your sources.' He shook again. 'Should I wait for help?' Like rising mist his answer appeared: 'Outlook not so good.'

He took a breath, rolled the tension out of his shoulders and shook again. 'Should I crawl down the unbelievably frightening dark tunnel which is probably full of poisonous spiders and angry bats?' He stopped shaking the phone, let it sit like a tiny bird cradled in his hand, and waited. His head dropped when he read the message. 'Signs point to yes.'

THE RELIEF PETRA had felt hearing Krishna's crackling voice on the phone had deserted her. Leaving the barrack room filled her with dread. Dane had insisted on heading up to where he'd last seen Carly, and despite Mary's protests Ed had agreed. Better to stick together, he'd reasoned. Dane was leading the four of them slowly, calling Carly's name in a raised whisper. His nervous caution made Petra feel all the more intimidated, as if deadly gangsters might leap out at any moment.

'Carly! Carly! If this is your idea of a joke, Carly
…'

'This doesn't feel right,' Petra said. 'Something's not right. Something's wrong.' The feeling of dread within her was reaching boiling point. Every step felt like the wrong move.

But Dane pushed onwards, calling Carly's name, Petra sweeping the one working torch around the black cavern ahead. She turned back to check that Ed and Mary were still with them, and in the moment of casting the torch beam behind her, Dane suddenly swore and fell. He'd tripped. Petra apologised and ran to help him. She looked down in the paltry light, Ed and Mary now with her, and saw Dane sprawled across something in their path. As he heaved himself up Petra saw a splayed body in jeans and sparkly pumps. She clasped her hand to her mouth and reeled back. Dane still hadn't realised. As he pushed himself up, Petra saw Carly's frayed pink denim jacket, but as the full horrifying image became clear she also saw that something was missing. Where Carly's face should have been, a huge rock was squashing the top of her chest, obliterating her head.

A scream pushed through Petra's fingers. Ed clasped Mary's face into his shoulder. It was only after a second or two that Dane realised what he was sitting on. His hands and chest were smeared in the blood of his fiancé. His eyes widened and mouth gaped, unable to make sound.

Ed was the first to speak. 'My God. Dane.'

'Carly ...' whispered Petra.

'C-Carly?' blurted Dane.

'Those fucking animals,' Ed said.

Mary stepped forward to look at the mess. 'I'm so sorry, Dane.'

Dane pushed himself off, and knelt beside Carly's corpse, unable to take in the abomination. Then he blurted, 'Did you see that?' He pointed to her feet. 'She moved!' Petra hadn't seen anything but Dane was convinced. 'She's alive!'

Thirteen

Krishna wasn't built for commando crawling and he certainly wasn't dressed for it. Wet shorts clung to his chafing thighs as his knees scuffed and slipped on the rough stone. His only light was the soft green glow of his phone's screen, held aloft in front of him, its night-vision camera working hard to pick up anything in the utter blackness. Stretched forwards on his belly, squirming, shuffling, panting and moaning, eventually the tight tunnel opened up enough for him to pull himself onto all fours. He glanced back. Nothing. Ahead: the same. His mind suddenly jumped to the worst-case scenario. What if this was a dead end? Was he trapped? He doubted he could shuffle backwards. If there was a rock fall behind him, he'd just spent a lot of effort crawling into his own coffin.

Fear spurred him on but almost immediately his knee sliced down a sharp ridge and made him yelp. Puffing and groaning, he managed to twist around to inspect it. The green phone screen just showed a blurred shape. The black blood of the cut was barely visible but he felt the warm slickness on his fingers.

He lay on his back, gathering his breath. He'd have to live with it. Just a scratch, he told himself. Then he felt something touch his shoulder. He twitched and felt a scratch on his neck. He yelped and twisted away and saw, illuminated by the green phone screen, a long, lean rat scurry across his belly. Before he could swipe at it, the matted rodent was at his knee, lapping and tugging at the fresh wound. In a blind panic Krishna pulled up his other foot and kicked at it with the back of his trainer. The rat dodged and the heel slammed into Krishna's sore knee. He howled in pain and lost his target, too fast, too sleek and too black to be seen.

'Fuck this,' he growled, and squirmed onto his stomach to crawl further into the Rock, his phone swishing ahead, more as a weapon than a visual aid. He didn't even see the blockage. His phone swiped against something with a hollow *clonk,* and then his head hit it.

Running his hands against it he felt a smooth, flat surface, not cold like rock, and too uniform to be natural. Flipping the phone, he saw in its dim screen-light that he'd reached the tunnel's end: plasterboard. He rapped it with his knuckles and the hollow knock was unmistakable. This tunnel had been boarded up.

He laughed. Damp plasterboard wouldn't present any barrier to him. With as much force as he could muster in his cramped space he slammed his fist into it, then howled again. It stayed firm, and now his knuckles were bleeding.

Furious, he reverse-crawled a few metres to the tunnel's widest point where he could turn his body around, a complicated, painful process that involved banging his head, swearing constantly, imagining rats in every crevice, and almost dislocating his spine. Eventually, with a roar of victory, he was on his back with his feet just yards from the stubborn barrier.

Shimmying his wet bottom forwards, crawling on his elbows, he soon felt the board against his feet. He pulled himself a little closer, his wet Hawaiian shirt now ridden up around his nipples. A couple of kicks made plenty of noise but the board stayed in place. He was certain it would give. He adjusted his position, pulled his scratched and bloody knees up as high as possible and slammed them forwards.

With an almighty, splintering crunch, he was through.

Like a massive, wet baby being born, Krishna's plump frame squeezed through the ragged hole. Wailing like the grotesque breeched infant he resembled, soon his tummy was through, red and angry, then his rumpled shirt gave way around his shoulders and his flailing feet fell forwards, pulling him out of the hole and slamming him down onto a hard floor.

He coughed, he spat, he cried a little. The floor felt cool and clean against his cheek. The acoustics had changed. Every spluttering noise he made sounded wider here, resonant, different to the claustrophobic hell above.

He'd made it. He was out. He was alive.

Blinking, he realised he could see. Only just, but there was light. He rolled onto his back, panting, shivering. He was in a room. Not a cave, or a tunnel, or a cavern. This was a *room*. It had proper smooth walls that rose up around him. It had a ceiling with an empty light cord hanging from it. Up there he saw the source of the light: narrow windows, like a basement has up at street level.

'You total legend,' he smiled. 'You've only gone and done it,' then sang, *"I see a bad moon risin' …"*, as he pulled himself to his feet. Sure enough, the dim grey light across the ceiling was moonlight, which meant one thing: he was all but free.

Around him was dusty chaos. The floor was strewn with crates and boxes, many of them split and spewing long-forgotten paperwork. A grey map of Europe hung on the wall. A crooked, torn picture of an old army general hung in a frame opposite. He saw a door at the end of the room and flew at it, but it held fast, bouncing him back into the dumping ground. He tried the light switch but it was dead. *Not dead: lacking a bulb,* he corrected, looking up at the empty cord. Scanning his surroundings more closely he realized that most of these boxes were from a house clearance, nothing to do with the original use of the room, which was some sort of military office from decades ago. Some of the crates were labelled in scrawled marker pen 'Bedroom 1', 'Living Room', once relevant to a long-lost home. In one called 'Kitchen' he rummaged for a tool to attack the door, finding spatulas, spoons, mouldy tea-towels and innumerable other useless tools never required by a locksmith. But he did find a box of light bulbs.

Pulling a crate underneath the light cord, he stood aloft to screw in the bulb. With a splintering crack the crate submitted to defeat and spilled him back to the floor, a sheaf of papers at his feet. He could make out in the darkness a newspaper staring up at him. He picked it up expecting it to be historically significant, declaring some military victory or 'peace in our time'. The headline wasn't memorable in global history: 'Two dead in mystery blaze.' He turned on his night-vision camera, which revealed the text in pin-sharp, green, high-definition.

It was a local paper, the *Chronicle & Echo,* from years ago. A faded photograph showed a gutted country house, blackened smears above its windows, a gaping, jagged scoop bitten from its roof. Under it Krishna read, 'Couple die in Pilkington Manor fire.'

'Pilkington ...' he murmured; a flicker of recognition.

Moving his phone across the text, certain details caught his eye: 'Chief fire officer reports the inferno appears to have been started with chemicals', 'police have not ruled out foul play', and 'they leave behind two teenage children'. He tossed it back to the pile of papers at his feet and moved to the door. Pushing it again, he examined the edges with his camera.

'Totally sealed,' he sighed. 'Impenetrable.'

Then as an afterthought he pulled on the handle. The door swung open. An unstoppable instinct made him check behind him in case anyone had seen his stupidity.

He stepped through into a completely dark room. Only the tiniest smear of depleted moonlight leaked in from the room behind, slowly extinguished by the closing door. Immediately, he stumbled into something that crashed with a metallic clatter like metal saucepans being knocked from a shelf. He swore, and reaching back to the edge of the door, his sweeping hand found a metal toggle light switch. Click, click – nothing.

He tapped his phone into life and cursed the battery indicator, now amber in colour and showing eleven per cent. He tried the torch one more time but the button still refused to activate it. Holding it aloft, peering at the night-vision image on the screen, he stood fast, bewildered by what he saw. The thing he'd bumped into was a gurney, a small hospital bed on a trolley, on which were piled metal trays of medical instruments. This was a laboratory or clinic of some sort. He was struggling to take it all in through his palm-sized screen; everywhere he held the phone, the image was a clutter of competing eras. It felt like a 1950s doctor's surgery, tatty, paint-peeled steel cabinets, a dusty clock hanging crooked on the wall, an antique-looking blood-pressure strap among the clutter on a vintage wooden desk. Yet among all this was modern medical paraphernalia: intravenous drip stands, discarded masks and latex gloves. And this was just in the metre or two around him.

'Christ,' he uttered, stepping into the eerie darkness. Then a thought struck him. He swiped his screen to select the normal camera. The room looked completely black without the night-vision setting, but the flash might still work. This spectacle was too weird *not* to share. Moving slowly, further into the centre of the lab, he held the phone up, unable to see anything but the icons around the black screen, and tapped the shutter circle. A bright flash filled the space, dazzling him for a second. For a moment the image of a blood-spattered steel table lay before him, before it reduced to a tiny box in the corner of the phone leaving the black screen ready for the next shot.

He tapped, *flash,* tapped again, *flash.* He was no longer looking at the screen, he was holding his breath, staring wide-eyed at the strobing horrors around him: large jars on shelves contained body parts, rows and rows of them, floating in yellow liquid, some decomposed husks, some fresh. One contained the dark-haired leg of an ape, its pink foot plump and waxy. A monkey's twisted arm filled another.

He kept tapping the screen, turned to the gurney and saw in the flashing white light that it was draped in polythene, caked with smears of dry blood. A gammy handsaw lay on it, the teeth holding chunks of flesh darkened by dried blood. Tangled in the blade was a wad of hair.

He spun around, adrenaline surging; another flash. His phone battery showed eight per cent. *Flash, flash,* panic rising. *Flash* – a chaotic storm of silhouettes swam in his blinking eyes, too many shapes for him to comprehend and then he saw it, on the far side of the laboratory, past IV stands and cabinets and endless clutter. One more flash of the camera clearly illuminated a pair of double doors.

Fourteen

Petra was witnessing a deep, hard-wired animal instinct. She'd seen it before. Gorillas carrying their floppy, lifeless baby for days. Whales refusing to let their dead calf sink, nudging it to the surface of the ocean again and again, sometimes for weeks. This was a new level of heartbreak. Tears poured down her cheeks as Dane knelt over Carly's corpse, frantically trying to save her.

'Carly! Carly, I'm here! Hang on!' He tried to lift the massive rock off her head but couldn't get a decent grip and looked to the others. 'Help me! C'mon, help me move this!'

Ed and Mary didn't move. Petra put her hand

on Dane's shoulder, trying to console him. 'Dane
…'

But he pulled her hand towards the boulder. 'C'mon Petra, help me.' She felt blood on her fingers. Carly's blood. Dane crouched at the rock and strapped his arms around it, straightening his back and heaving. 'Carly! I'm here.' With a grunt the stone rose a few centimetres. Petra saw a curl of blonde hair underneath it before the boulder slipped from Dane's blood-wet hands and dropped with a sickening wet crunch. Ed winced and Mary looked away.

Petra leaned forward, putting her arm around Dane's shoulders. 'Leave her, Dane. It's too late.'

'No! No … I …' He broke down, hopeless, gasping sobs echoing from the walls around them. 'Who'd do something like this?'

Petra looked at Ed. He was looking at Mary. 'Smugglers,' he said. 'They'll stop at nothing.'

Petra said, 'Dane, we've got to go.'

'I'm not leaving her. No way.'

Mary stepped forward. 'Dane, we can't do any-thing for her. We must leave.'

Her instruction was met with anger. 'I'm not leaving Carly to rot in this hole!'

KRISHNA WAS PANICKING. He barged his way towards the doors in complete darkness, bumping against cabinets, tangling in an old office chair, clattering his way to freedom. Pushing hopelessly at cold walls, he ran his hands wide looking for a door to swing open. His fingers felt the frame, then painted wood, but nothing moved as he shoved. He stepped across and felt further over, searching for a bolt or handle when the back of his hand touched something soft and cool at hip height. He jerked it back. Sparing his phone's battery, he allowed himself one more camera flash. He just had to find the bolt securing these double doors. He raised the phone, pointed and tapped. A bright white light filled the room, less than a second but long enough. Long enough to burn an image on his retina. Slumped against the corner, he glimpsed what his hand had touched: a mutilated corpse gazed up at him from black, hollow eye sockets. Both its legs had been dismembered at the knee, stubby limbs splayed wide, ragged wounds turned to blackened crusts, the hands lying peacefully at its crotch, the head lolling back, jaw twisted.

Krishna heaved, his abdomen cramping, then he roared and threw himself at the doors, which rattled but held fast. Sweeping his hand in front of him, he found cold metal, a latch at eye level. Trembling fingers found the fat lever; he yanked it but it didn't budge. He pushed it with his palm and the door swung wide, tumbling him into grey light.

Stumbling forwards, he dodged and spun, adrenaline twitching his every nerve. The *clack* of the heavy door latching shut behind him made him jump with fright. Panting, sweating, he was alone. Gulping dry air in his clammy mouth, he quickly took in his surroundings. This was a corridor, a short, windowless passage with a couple of dirty plastic domed skylights in the ceiling. The brick walls had dark grey, peeling paint up to waist height, then a single filthy white line, and a lighter grubby grey paint above that, the two-tone hallmark of a 1960s municipal building.

He lunged forwards towards the opposite end of the passage. In the gloom his hands found a large, rusting steel door. He recognised it immediately as a blast-trap door like those Ed had explained that afternoon. He pulled at its thick, corroded handle, like a slug of scaffold pipe welded to an impenetrable steel slab. The door didn't even creak. He bounced his shoulder against it but the harder he barged the harder it hit back. Furious, he hollered, 'AAAAARGH' and kicked the metal door until his scream turned into a yell of pain, each deafening impact sounding like the banging of a wartime field gun.

PETRA FROZE. They all did. Even Dane hushed his sobs at the echoing *BOOM, BOOM, BOOM* rolling around the tunnels. 'Shit, they're still here,' she said. 'We've gotta go!'

'I'm bringing Carly.'

'What?' Mary exclaimed. 'We haven't got time! They could be on us at any moment!'

Ed attempted to reason with him. 'Dane, we can't stay here. It's not safe. We'll come back for her.'

A moan of agony came from deep within Dane as he flopped onto Carly's lifeless belly and sobbed. He hugged her around the waist and whispered through choking coughs, 'I'm sorry. I'm so sorry. I love you.'

'Dane! Move!' Ed ordered.

'NO!' shouted Dane spinning round. It happened in the blink of an eye, almost too fast and too grotesque for Petra to take in. Dane's strength was such that as he rounded on Ed, a snagging, crunching sound came from the floor – a sickening, sinew-snapping tear, like wrenching a stubborn leg from a roast chicken. Carly's immovable head had almost detached from her corpse.

'Oh God,' Petra gulped, clasping her hand to mouth. Dane dropped the body in shock at what he'd done and Mary reeled backwards.

The only person remaining cool was Ed. 'Dane. We need to go.'

Coughing, retching, spit dribbling from his drooping mouth, he quietly asked, 'Go where?' His quiet whine chilled Petra. She knew that voice. The empty croak of lost hope. Dane was resigned to give up and die right there.

Fifteen

Breathless, stinking, and with the rancid smell of that blind, hacked-up, composting corpse still clinging to the back of his throat, Krishna was trapped. He leaned his back against the old blast-trap door and cast his eyes to the ceiling. The two grey rectangles of the dirty plastic skylights were the only shapes visible in the darkness. Slowly, his brain realised that, like the slotted windows in the dump room he'd broken into, they must be lit by the moon. He was in a brick corridor linking some sort of decrepit military bunker with the Rock. What the hell had gone on here? And where were his friends?

That was when he saw it: something irregular in

the painted line along the middle of the corridor wall. 'You're joking,' he sighed. He'd blundered right past it. A fire exit in the side of the corridor, painted exactly like the walls, a push bar across its middle. He placed his hands gently on the bar, unable to truly believe it would open. He leaned his forehead on the door, mouthed a silent prayer, and pushed.

A click, a creak, and a gust of fresh air hit his face.

'Thank you, God.'

He stepped into moonlight, a gentle warm breeze and the heavy scent of honeysuckle and wild jasmine. He was free.

Looking around, he saw that the building behind him was literally a bunker – he could barely see its edges under a thick wilderness of shrubs. Ahead of him the mountainous Rock rose steeply from his feet. He checked his phone for a signal. Five per cent battery. He held it high, squinting at the screen. Zero bars.

'Piece of shit.'

He started climbing. He would get altitude, get a signal, get help. The grassy bank on this undisturbed face of the Rock was steady but rising fast. In less than a minute he was doubled over, panting for breath, his cut knee zinging with pain.

Looking up at the pale grey outline, he could see high above him the path that led around to the tunnel entrance where he'd seen the police car, where just hours ago he and his friends had laughed at stupid selfies and at the weird old guy checking their passports.

There was no way he could climb up to there from here. Even in the dim light a sudden absence of grass and shrubs showed that a steep, rocky cliff blocked his route. Up to his right, though, there was hope. A ledge, higher up this grassy slope, would surely give him the height to get a phone signal.

He lifted his throbbing leg, planted it in the damp grass and pushed. Soon he was grabbing at bushes, feet slipping on shale. The climb was too hard, too much. What looked like an achievable trek from below had become perilous. He glanced back down and a whimper slipped from his lips. He checked the phone screen: four per cent; no signal. He blew his cheeks out a couple of times, steeling himself.

'C'mon, big man. You've got this.'

The giddying height he'd already achieved boosted his resolve. He looked up at the ledge. 'Just there! Just – up – there!' Scraping, sliding, grasping and groaning, he hauled his weight through brambles and bushes, steeper up the incline, occasionally sending showers of grit and shale rattling off the rocks below.

Mud, blood and sweat smeared his face, legs and belly as he reached the protruding ledge. He flung his arms over the top, grabbed fistfuls of thick, wiry weeds, and pulled himself to safety.

For a minute or so he just lay there, sprawled, his gasping lungs like a slowing steam engine, his face squashed against the dark moist ground. It smelled of earth, of life. He felt an overwhelming peace.

Gathering himself for his task, he opened his eyes and tentatively got to his knees. With a steadying hand against the rising slab of limestone beside him, he carefully stood up. He chanced a look down over the lip of the ledge but the drop was so dizzying he lurched back against the cold rock face.

Then a thought occurred. *How the hell am I gonna get down?*

He shook his head, emptying it of doubt. Maybe they'll send a helicopter. But only if …

He extended his hand toward the heavens and squeezed the phone into life. The screen lit. 'Still four per cent,' he murmured. 'Please. You can do this.' He was looking at the dormant corner of the screen, which showed his network provider but no signal. He waited.

Bing. One slender bar of signal. He was saved.

PETRA WAS HELPING Dane to his feet. He was unable to look at Carly now, his eyes scrunched up, squeezed tears tracking down his cheeks. 'That's it,' she gently reassured him. 'Come with me. Let's get to safety and then the police can sort this out. There's nothing you can do now.' To her surprise he hugged her, burying his face in her shoulder. She squeezed him hard. He was taut. He was broken.

Mary seemed immune to the grotesque mess at her feet and was squinting ahead, past Carly and down the passage. 'Let's just get to the next crossroads because then we've got options.'

She stepped past Petra and Dane, ignored Carly's splintered, blood-sodden remains, cracked a glow-stick and walked. Ed trod past them in her tow. Petra released her grip on Dane, who sniffled and gave her arm a squeeze. She led him onwards, after the others, away from the girl he had loved.

Almost immediately, the four of them were at a crossroads. Ed quickly surveyed the options and said, 'Forwards. This way.' They strode on but as Petra and Dane crossed the junction she put her arm across his chest, slowing him down. A gap grew between the green glow of Ed and Mary and their own dim torchlight. Dane shrugged at her, wondering why she was holding him up.

She glanced ahead then looked into his wet eyes and said, 'Dane, I don't think we're lost.'

He wiped his nose on the sleeve of his T-shirt. 'What?'

She shushed him.

'Petra, we're very fucking lost!' He started to walk but Petra grabbed his arm.

'Wait. If we're lost, why would she say "Let's go to the crossroads" and then immediately *there's a crossroads?* What if they're fucking with us?'

He strolled on. The green light of their leaders' glow-stick was getting smaller. 'There are crossroads everywhere,' he said.

'And what about the barrack room?' she spat in a hoarse whisper. 'He knew where that was!'

'You're paranoid. We're all scared, Petra. This has been … fucking awful. Let's just go.' He broke away from her grip and jogged ahead to meet Ed and Mary. Dragging the weight of a heavy heart, Petra pulled herself after him, towards the green glow – ahead, three people she hardly knew; behind, the only one she'd counted as a friend, growing cold in the dark.

Sixteen

'You little beauty,' smiled Krishna, his phone held high like an Olympic athlete proudly clasping a flaming torch for the world to see. His screen told him it was almost two a.m., and the moon, almost full, was directly overhead. The lightest wisps of cloud shrouded her light, but Krishna could clearly see a monochrome landscape below him. The flickering lights of the Spanish coast were just a thin, black strip of sea away. He could hear the distant rasp of a moped drift across from the mainland. There was life out there. People. People who could help.

He drew breath, tapped his phone's screen and brought up the last number dialled. 'Dane' appeared across the screen. Before his thumb could tap the green button, a shriek erupted from nearby, a deafening screech from behind and somewhere above him. He ducked in fright, spun round and looked up to see a blaze of white fur across a black shape hurtling towards him from the sky.

He threw his arms up and reeled backwards. The ape glanced off his chest at the same moment that Krishna's foot scuffed beyond the ridge and into fresh air. His arms windmilled, his jettisoned phone flew high into the air. His wide, panic-filled eyes saw the ape standing in the grey light, watching him fall, lips curled back in a clownish grin, one arm missing. Then there was sky, rushing wind, the gentle moon above. There was a small flurry of birds erupting from shrubs, a deep, loud, crunching thud, and the ripple of chatter from disturbed rock apes. There was the buzz of the distant moped drifting away. Then there was silence.

As PETRA CAUGHT UP with the others, Ed picked up the pace. For a man on a bent prosthetic leg, he was making good ground. 'This is it, it's down here!' He sounded excited and Petra was almost at a jog to keep up with them. 'It's just a bit further. I know where we are!'

'Oh, thank God,' said Dane.

Petra was looking around, trying to see if any of this looked familiar. It didn't *feel* like the way they'd come in. Turning the corner, they reached a large metal blast-trap door. Mary turned to them, beaming. 'We're here!' Petra looked at Dane, who smiled back at her, tearful with relief.

The thick, rusty steel door was secured by a tangle of chains, which Ed released with expert ease. A scraping clatter filled the passage as he shoved the door, which opened about halfway before grinding to a stop. They all pushed through the gap and Petra found herself in a new place.

This wasn't the Rock. There was enough dim light in here to see that the walls were painted bricks. Mary leaned her shoulder against the metal door, grinding it back into place.

Dane was looking around, up at the high ceiling with two grubby plastic skylights. 'Where *are* we?'

'Relax,' smiled Mary. 'It's over.' She stood with her back to the corridor wall, beckoning them to follow Ed to the far end. He had pulled a jangling keyring from his pocket and Petra heard the decisive *clack* of a lock. One of two double doors swung wide open revealing a black void beyond.

'This way,' grinned Ed.

Mary led the way through, smiling encouragingly to Dane. 'Follow me.'

As Petra stepped past Ed he said, 'I'll throw the power on,' and followed her into the darkness.

BAM! The door slammed, engulfing them in black.

'Dane? Ed? What the fuck? Where are we?' Petra heard a *crack* and with a hum of electrical surge the room was suddenly brightly lit. She cried out and staggered back against the door. Her eyes could barely take in the array of horrors, clinically illuminated around her. Rotting limbs were strewn among discarded green surgical gowns and upturned medical equipment. Jars of remains, animal and human, lined the walls on haphazard wooden shelves. Rusting steel cabinets stood crooked alongside shining steel IV stands.

On a gurney behind Ed lay the corpse of a girl in her twenties: red hair, still in summer tourist clothes, a crop-top vest and shorts. Petra retched at the waxy, sunken features. The arm nearest her hung from the gurney like the broken hand of a clock, a Disney Tigger tattoo near the shoulder.

The other arm had been severed just below the shoulder and was attached to a different, withered, blackened, decomposing arm. At the wrist, the limb had rotted to such an extent that the bone was visible.

'Holy fuuuuuck!' uttered Dane.

'Excuse the mess,' smiled Ed. He was relaxed, stepping carefully through the debris while Mary busied herself with pulling on surgical gloves and organising a tray of instruments.

Petra turned to flee, saw the slumped, blind corpse staring up from her feet, and screamed. Ed slid across the doorway, blocking her path, and pushed her back into the room. She yelled past him, 'HELP! HELP!' while Ed rolled his eyes.

Dane, paralysed with fear and confusion, gazed at his surroundings uttering baffled questions. 'Where? What is this place?'

The fractured pieces of the puzzle fell rapidly into place for Petra. A fire inside her roared: adrenaline, fear, fury. 'I knew it! I fucking knew something was wrong! You're not helping us! You're … you're … what the fuck *are* you?' Dane's dumbfounded face was slack while Petra blasted, 'You knew all along where you were leading us!' But Ed just smirked.

Petra didn't see Mary coming and Dane was too slow to react. A lunge, a swing, and a plastic syringe was plunged into her neck. Petra grabbed at the pain but the needle was hanging limp from her flesh, its load already delivered. She turned, her knees buckled; Mary stood above her, a victorious sneer on her tight lips. Collapsing, swallowed by darkness, the last thing Petra heard was Ed saying, 'Lovely work, angel,' and the distant, hollow reply from Mary:

'Shame the blonde one didn't go down so easily.'

Seventeen

With the same catapulting violence of a catatonic drug user being resuscitated with an adrenaline shot to the heart, Dane sprang to life, startled, angry and confused. He launched himself at Mary, who squirmed sideways out of his reach. As she dodged away Ed lunged, as if yanked by a wire, slamming the corpse-laden gurney into the small of Dane's back. The impact threw him against the wall a second before he felt the spasm of agony.

He spun around, roaring in pain, a clumsy giant compared to nimble Mary. Off balance, pressed to the wall by the trolley, he tried to steady himself as he fell forwards. His outstretched hand pressed on the exposed stomach of the putrid cadaver and with a slimy squelch pushed straight through. A cold, slippy spinal column filled his hand. He jerked it back, smeared with noxious decay.

Mary and Ed shared a laugh, enjoying Dane's grotesque slapstick. He raised his foot and with the precision and strength of a mountaineer planted it on the edge of the gurney and launched it like a speeding train straight back at Ed, barrelling him to the floor. Dane was back at the door in a flash, but so was Mary, just a couple of paces behind him as he slammed the latch with his palm and bashed the door open. Without a backward glance he wrenched at the handle, slamming it into Mary's face – but something stopped it.

A piercing scream filled his ears and he looked down to see that the bottom of the swing door had wedged hard against Mary's open toe sandal, ripping off her big toenail. It was jutting vertically, pooling with blood. He looked past her, saw Petra unconscious on the floor, Ed clambering to his feet … and he ran.

In the empty passage he saw his escape and exploded through the fire door, slamming it shut behind him, muting Mary's murderous ravings. Neither of his pursuers would be incapacitated for long so he ran straight up the grassy bank, putting distance between him and the bunker below. Panting, his mouth dry, his body soaked with sweat, blood and fetid remains, he looked back down. The door remained closed. No movement at all.

Panic ebbed into guilt. He could save himself. He was free. But what about Petra? He swore. He had to go back, didn't he? His stomach cramped at the thought. He couldn't go back in there. Not without help.

'KRISHNA!' he yelled, not really expecting any response.

The dark grey night remained quiet.

'Where the hell are you?'

Krishna was closer than he thought, cold, lifeless and alone, but the Rock kept its secret.

If I don't go back for Petra, she's dead for sure, he thought. But what if she *didn't* die? That would be worse. She'd tell of how Dane was there one minute, gone when she awoke. How would that look when the police started asking questions?

'Police!'

Scanning the hillside in the gloom he worked

out that although the easiest route up was to the right, it was in entirely the wrong direction for the main entrance. The tunnel mouth where the police car was parked was a short climb up to the left. A steep ascent, but significantly quicker than running all the way back to Gibraltar town – plus, Ed and Mary could never make that climb.

Running some sections, conquering steep, almost vertical rock with the last drops of his energy, finding footholds and finger-cracks with experienced instinct, he was soon hauling himself up onto the high pathway he and his friends had walked only hours ago. The exhausted figure dragging itself around the bend to the tunnel entrance was a shadow of the athlete he'd looked back then.

But there it was, silhouetted where it had been earlier, the distinctive shape of the police car. He staggered towards it, picking up pace. Behind misted windows, listening to the radio, pouring a steaming drink from a flask, was a police officer. Dane almost tripped and slammed his hands against the car window, making the man jolt with fright and shower himself with hot coffee.

'Mierda!' he cried, but when he saw the blood-smeared hands on the window and Dane's haggard face, his fury turned to alarm.

'Help!' shouted Dane at the glass. 'Come! Rapido!' he pulled at the door handle, then at the policeman's sleeve, dragging him from his warm, muggy den.

'What the hell?' complained the cop. He was a slight, gaunt man with dark, searching, suspicious eyes. When he shone his torch at Dane he took a step back. 'Dios mío! You hurt?'

'Come with me! You must come!'

'Calm, Eengleesh. Slow.'

'You've got to help us! Down there, a bunker. There's a … they've *killed* someone!'

He placed his hand on Dane's shoulder. 'You're safe now. I'm Officer Jurado. Tell me, slowly. Tell me what happened.'

'Two people, they've killed Carly. My Carly! And others. Dead! Er … muerto! Come on!' Dane tried to pull Jurado down the path with him.

'Espere, espere, hold on. I should call for help, no? How many are there?'

'Two! I just … for fu – we don't have time! Quick! Rapido! They still have Petra. We need to go!'

The sluggish cop thought for a second or two and then seemed convinced by Dane's panic. He

168

quickly reached into the car and pulled out a clip of ammo from the glove box, slapped it into the base of the pistol on his hip and said, 'Lead the way.'

PETRA'S HEAD HURT. A fuzzy, buzzing headache which she could almost hear inside her skull. She lay still, giving herself a few seconds to come round. *Eyes closed,* she told herself. *Play dead.*

She felt something pulling at her ankle. Quickly, the memories tumbled through her mind: the trap, the deceit, the macabre death-lab, Ed's chilling acceptance of the horror, his even more insane girlfriend. And Carly. Poor, poor Carly. Murdered by this fucking psycho-bitch. Her last memory before the blackness had swamped her, Mary's smiling voice gloating at Carly's death, swam around her head. She resisted the urge to open her eyes, leap up and wreak bloody revenge. *Shhhhhh, Petra,* she commanded herself. *Play dead.*

The tugging was at her hips now and she realised she was being strapped down. *Gurney restraints,* she calculated. She could hear breathing but her captors weren't talking. She channelled all her willpower into slowing her own lungs. *Pretend to sleep!* she yelled in her head. Then slowly, almost imperceptibly, she tensed her arms.

Predictably, that's where the next strap fell, across her arms and chest. She had no idea whether this old escapologists' trick ever worked, but she'd seen it on a Houdini documentary once. Tense when restrained so your body is bigger. Relax and the restraints will slacken.

At least, that was the theory.

Click!

Her ears pricked. The person strapping her down suddenly fell still. There was someone outside. She heard Mary whisper, 'Ed,' but was quickly shushed. In Petra's mind she placed Mary over to her right, beyond her feet. Ed's 'Shush' came from right above her chest. She felt the strap-tail drop and heard him walk away. She heard muffled voices, also trying not be heard. She guessed she was near the swing doors, and from the snippet she heard it sounded like men's voices on the other side.

Thank God! The fucking cavalry. Dane, Krishna, the police with any luck. How was this going to play out? If Ed and Mary were squaring up for a fight, and God knows they weren't squeamish when it came to violence, she did *not* want to be strapped to a trolley-bed in the middle of their suicidal swansong. She was already a witness. Why wasn't she already dead?

She heard the swing door give a tiny squeak and the latch hold. One of the men was gently pushing it. Then, a *crack,* like a blunt axe hitting a tree, a yelping groan, and the door rattled as something slid down it.

She tensed against her straps but quickly resumed her bogus coma. The push latch flicked, she heard the door shove open, pushing against a blockage which eventually shifted. Then she heard Ed, his voice just beyond the open door. 'Ah … the one that got away.'

'No loose ends, Mr Pilkington.' The voice had a thick Spanish accent that fitted none of the gangsters in Petra's mind. 'You need to be more careful. I saw some guys slip away an hour ago. Midnight boat to Africa kind of guys. What if Mr Eengleesh here had bumped into *them* …'

'We did.'

'No!'

'Indeed. It turned into a bit of a gathering. As much of a surprise to us as it was to them. Wasn't really accounting for all that. There's a clean-up required. One dead gangster and a girl. She needs to … you know. Disappear.'

'Mierda. You are not paying me enough.'

'Ha! How's that yacht of yours?'

'Fishing boat. Not that I do much fishing.'

Petra heard the ruffling of cash, and Ed mutter, 'I'm sure the fish will thank you for another of your midnight deliveries, Jurado.' She heard a pat on the arm. 'Come on, you do all right. You relish the credit. "Local cop finds remains of foiled smuggler." You'll dine out on this.'

Cop! Petra's mind raced, her eyelids barely a flicker. This was a *policeman?* Her mind reeled at the scale of this elaborate trap. Were they ever really lost, or just being shepherded to slaughter?

She heard grimacing, heaving noises, and Jurado say, 'He's a heavy one.'

A clatter of equipment being kicked and pushed aside, and with a final grunting heave, gulping breaths of relief. Then footsteps, and Jurado's voice right above her. 'Who is this?'

'No one. Forget it.'

Jurado laughed. 'I think this one be no use to you, amigo.'

'I do hope you're not suggesting what I think you're suggesting,' Mary said from the other side of the room.

'Explain, Jurado,' Ed said. 'Why no good? Do tell.'

'No, no, I just mean … y'know, she's … not 'cause she's black. I just, y'know …'

There was a pause. Petra could hear that the man named Jurado was nervous.

'Because she's a woman?' asked Mary.

'Yes! That's what I was saying. This one is a woman. No use for you.'

'Bravo, Officer,' Ed drawled. 'We'll make an enlightened 21st-century man of you yet. She's a black woman. Mixed race, actually. Might still need her. She's healthy, fit.'

'Not that fit,' Mary scowled.

'You know what I mean. Too good to waste. For now, at least.'

Jurado turned away and Petra heard his voice change. 'Seriously, Mr. Pilkington, this man is … a little bigger than you. No offence. Is this really the one, you think?'

'I hope so,' Ed replied. 'I hope so.'

Eighteen

Minutes passed. Petra slept, as far as her captors were aware. After the policeman left she didn't hear much talking from Ed and Mary, just soft feet moving across the floor, the occasional click, snap and ruffle of movement. Eventually, once she'd established that they were both further down the room, off to her right, her curiosity was too much.

Gently, slowly, with the tiniest of flickers, she risked lifting one eyelid a crack. She instantly realised that her body had been strapped with her head at the wall and her feet facing straight down the laboratory towards them. She stifled a gasp at the blurred view she glimpsed. Ed was wearing green surgical scrubs and around his neck hung a paper surgeon's mask. He was adjusting the position of a gurney beneath a fluorescent light that hung from the flaking, grubby ceiling on rusted chains.

She closed her eye. *Stay calm!* Was that the gurney the redheaded girl had been on? Where was that poor soul now?

'I told you not to go inside the Rock at night.' It was Ed. She heard a struggle and opened an eye again.

Dane! He'd just woken to find himself undressed to his underwear and strapped to a gurney, and was thrashing against the restraints. 'You fucking psycho! I'm gonna rip your fucking head off!'

Ed simply stood watching him, a safe pace back. He was on the other side of the bed from Petra's vantage point and she could see him smiling. Mary, her back to Petra, was opposite Ed preparing an injection, sucking fluid into a syringe from an upturned vial.

'Shhhhh, now,' purred Ed, which made Dane thrash some more. Mary handed Ed the needle and Petra saw him stop as he took her hand. He pulled her gloved fingers gently under the light, admiring a ring slipped over the blue latex. Even with her eye half-open Petra saw the sparkle of diamonds and a lavender glint of tanzanite.

'That really suits you, darling,' Ed said.

'You fucking bitch!' raged Dane. 'You had it all along! You stole it!'

Mary smiled. 'I was given it. Your girlfriend said "please take it" – didn't she, Ed?'

'Affirmative.'

Dane twisted and roared. Ed calmly squirted a tiny jet of fluid from the upturned syringe and, completely ignoring Dane's bellowing, said to Mary, 'That was a stroke of genius, angel – pocketing the ring, spotting the grid. I was genuinely looking for it until you quietly led me away. The discreet mastermind, hatching a plan while everyone's nose was on the ground.'

She leaned across Dane's contorted body and kissed Ed gently on the lips. 'You're welcome. He seemed too good a specimen to waste.'

Ed gave an admiring nod to the climber's tense physique and placed the needle against Dane's arm, but Mary gently placed her hand on Ed's, stopping him.

'HELP!' shouted Dane, but Mary remained calm.

'Wait, Ed.'

'What?'

'PETRA! WAKE UP!' screamed Dane, which made Petra quickly shut her eye.

'No anaesthetic,' she heard Mary say.

'He'll scream the place down.'

'He tried to run. He needs to suffer.'

Petra heard the panting, panicking Dane say, 'What? HELP!' and opened her eyes just a smidge.

Ed seemed to be considering Mary's request, so she pressed on: 'He hurt me, Edward. You're supposed to protect me.'

'What about the noise? It's nearly dawn. Someone will hear.'

'HELLLLP!' shouted the now hoarse Dane, no longer thrashing, half sobbing.

'You're right, my darling,' smiled Mary. 'Of course you're right.'

Petra saw Mary place a finger and thumb on Dane's throat, as if measuring his Adam's apple, like she was checking something. Dane looked at her, dumbstruck.

'What?' she asked him. '*Now* you stop screaming?'

'HELLLP MEEEEE PLEEEEEASE!' he cried.

Mary smiled, adjusted her fingers and said, 'Thank you,' before swiftly clasping a scalpel in her hand and resting it vertically on Dane's throat. With a precise smack of her palm onto the clenched fist, the blade sank an inch through skin and cartilage.

Dane's cries became a hoarse, guttural, wheezing shower of blood. Petra flinched, winced and prayed she hadn't been noticed. Dane's eyes were saucers of terror; his open throat coughed puffs of blood onto Mary's scrubs.

'It's only your vocal cords, Dane,' she smiled, stroking his fringe with the tenderness of a comforting nurse. 'You'll live.' Then her face dropped, all warmth banished. 'For now.'

Petra's head was clearing, the anaesthetic hangover fading. She risked a minuscule squirm to test the tension of her restraints. Casting a downward glance, she could see that the fibre strap on her chest was held by a metal pull-tag, like a luggage strap. Her hand was lying right next to her hip, so without looking she let her tentative fingers silently explore the strap across her waist, and felt the same cold metal of a similar latch. With a gentle push of her thumb she felt the belt slip, the pressure on her hips release.

Then she saw Ed. He'd turned away from Dane's gurney and had returned holding a polished, shiny medical saw. Dane emitted a wheezing, empty screech, sending a mist of bloody air ballooning up from his neck. 'Wha ... what are you doing?' he stammered in a rasping, bubbling whisper.

'This might hurt a little,' Ed replied.

Mary pulled the lid from a black marker pen with her teeth, leaned over and drew a dotted line around Dane's right leg, just below the knee. Petra saw Dane twisting and straining against his straps, which only made Ed pull them even tighter.

'No! Please!' coughed Dane's breathless mouth.

Petra watched Ed place the saw blade on Dane's leg, carefully lining it up. With a jerk, he pushed the barbed steel teeth through tensed flesh. Dane howled a hopeless blast of empty air, spattering speckles of blood onto them both.

'Stop!' Dane pleaded. 'Stop, you sick fuck! You're crazy!'

In an explosion of fury, before Ed could continue, Mary snatched up her scalpel and drove it through the back of Dane's hand, causing a blow-hole fountain of blood-spray as he tried to scream.

'Crazy?' she snapped. 'You really have no idea. Ed is about to make history, you dumb cretin. A lifetime of being told human limb grafts are impossible, that no immunosuppressant is capable of stopping the body's rejection, and yet here we are. Here *you* are, about to change all that. This genius –' she looked at Ed with adoring eyes '– will change the world.'

Dane was panting, sweating, looking in horror at the scalpel protruding from his hand.

'Well, I don't know about genius,' Ed smiled modestly.

'You *are*, darling. They said it couldn't be done.'

'She's right, Dane. You are about to make history. Back when no one would listen, I *knew* that what we're about to do was possible. Unfortunately the very institutes that were supposed to be supporting my research were funded by the industries that have invested millions in prosthetic limbs. No one was going to wave goodbye to that cash cow.'

'Corporate greed, Dane, you know how it is,' Mary sighed.

'And besides,' shrugged Ed, 'all the research money goes into cancer.'

'Fucking cancer.' There was a beat of silence and then Mary's mood brightened. 'But this is it! They said it could never be done, and God knows it hasn't been easy. But Dane … you're the special one. The last transplant so *nearly* worked.' She looked at a black plastic body bag slumped against the far door like a bin-liner waiting to be taken out to the trash. Petra quickly joined the dots – the redhead girl who'd been lying in her place. Victim of their last botched surgery.

'You see, Dane –' Ed was waving the saw at Dane as he preached his message '– if you had died here tonight inside the Rock, running from gangsters and smugglers, you'd be a nobody. You'd have achieved nothing. But giving up this leg … you're *something* Dane. You're *proof.* Part of something that will last forever.'

Petra was watching everything through half-closed eyes, as still as a sleeping statue. Any movement now would be seen. Dane was sobbing, weak and defeated. Ed pulled a stainless steel IV stand on wheels nearer to the table. A clear polythene bag hung from the loop in the stand, and Petra could see large, handwritten letters on its label: ISARC-13.

'You should be proud,' Mary said, looking down at Dane. 'You'll be the evidence that ISARC works. Immunosuppressive Anti-Rejection Chemical. Literally a world-changing innovation. Once Ed's proved it's effective here, he can go public, recreate it in a research lab, let the world discover his brilliance at a transplant hospital, and as if from nowhere he's vindicated, rich, famous and –'

'And all on my own. Edward Pilkington: he was right all along.'

'All on his own! My Edward. And all you can do is whine about your leg.'

Desperate, Dane hoarsely whispered, 'You're mad! Mad! And stupid! You think you can graft my leg onto yours? You're going to have to chop your own fucking stump off!'

Ed smiled at Mary and said, 'You see? I told you he was brighter than he looked.'

'We're prepped for that, smart-arse,' Mary said in a withering tone. She gestured to an empty gurney behind her, draped in fresh polythene.

'Surgery?' rasped Dane 'We'll die of blood loss!'

Petra breathed slowly, full of pride for Dane, manfully attempting to engage these lunatics, talk his way to some sort of escape.

'You're right,' Ed said. 'Death from blood loss is a real possibility … for you. I'm lucky, though. I have a ready supply of matched blood right here. Thanks to my twin.'

Mary leaned across the gurney and pecked a kiss onto Ed's lips. 'Mummy and Daddy would be so proud of what we've achieved.'

'You're right,' he murmured looking into her eyes. 'What happened at home will have all been worth it.'

With barely a beat to compose himself, Ed threw his weight into sawing at Dane's leg. A chaotic explosion of rasping, thrashing and hacking surrounded the table. Petra couldn't watch, but with Mary and Ed so consumed in their grim task, and Dane putting up such a fight, she stole her chance. Twisting her hips, she wriggled up the gurney enough to slip her left arm free. Glancing at the carnage to check that she had not been noticed, she reached over and undid her straps.

She lay still. The scene of the amputation had grown quiet. Dane had passed out. Ed paused to wipe his brow like a workman sawing a stubborn piece of timber. No longer needed to hold down Dane, Mary had stepped away from the table and was casually inserting a bloodline catheter into her arm. Petra watched her secure the needle across her vein with tape and saw the floppy tube turn dark with blood, slowly filling a bag in her hand.

'How long before you can walk on this?' Mary asked, in the same idle way she might have asked about the weather. 'I really want to take that holiday we've been promising ourselves.'

Ed furrowed his brow in thought. 'Five weeks? Four if the ISARC is as effective as I expect.' He leaned into his task again. The rasp of saw on bone gave way to easier strokes through sinew and flesh. 'Finally,' he muttered as the last piece of skin snapped and the leg dropped loose, a massive pool of dark, warm blood dripping onto the floor.

'Is he dead yet?' asked Mary.

She never got a reply. Like a panther snaring an unsuspecting lamb, Petra was on her. Gripping the trolley frame for leverage, she catapulted herself from horizontal to a mid-air lunge in the blink of an eye, wrenching the bloodline from the bag as she engulfed her prey. Mary screamed, the flapping tube spraying her blood across them both. Petra had her pinned down but saw Ed snatching the saw from Dane's leg and clambering around the table.

Petra's brief distraction was all Mary needed. From the medical detritus around them she scooped an old, stained scalpel and plunged it into Petra's thigh. An animal scream roared from within Petra, pain shooting through her. Planting a knee in Mary's chest and drenched in her blood, Petra clawed at the space above them, finding the edge of a battered steel shelving cabinet.

Pulling like an athlete twice her size, she hauled the shelves towards them. As they tilted she pulled harder, hoisting herself off Mary as dozens of jars of chemicals rained down. The noise was spectacular: smashing glass, deafening steel, and the screams, the agonising wails of Mary underneath it all.

Somewhere among all this Ed was shouting, 'Noooooo!' but Petra was standing fast, eyes locked on Mary. The woman was slapping, wiping and flapping in agony as a cocktail of chemicals blistered and scorched her skin. Her scrubs were smouldering as they shrunk and clung to her hissing flesh.

Ed flung the gurney out of the way and leapt at Petra with the bloody saw. She stooped, avoiding the blade, and swung a kick at Ed's knee. There was a splintering crack, but no shouts of pain from Ed. His prosthetic leg had taken the impact and was buckled, half attached and sticking out from his knee at a grotesque angle.

Off balance, he stumbled back into the wall. Petra saw disbelief in his face, shock at how quickly the tables had turned. Still upright, Ed picked up some sort of medical retractor, a length of steel with a hook at one end, and swiped at Petra with it. She ducked, but not quickly enough to avoid it completely. It glanced off her head and planted itself in the IV bag of ISARC-13, tearing it open and spilling its contents.

'What have you done?' he gasped. 'Years … *years* of my life. WHAT HAVE YOU DONE?!'

Mary was shoving her way out of the smashed shelving, mopping herself with old scrubs, but Petra saw her chance. She flew across the obliterated laboratory to the swing door, smacked the latch and pushed. Panting, caked in blood, she glanced back. Mary was on her knees, blistering welts on her face, looking for Ed. He was lost, disconnected, shaking his head, unable to comprehend the ruinous end of his dream. Dane was pale. Dane was still. Dane was dead.

Gritting her teeth, Petra clasped the scalpel in her fist. With a grunt of pain she tore it from her thigh, dropped it and ran.

Nineteen

Jurado was back near his patrol car, checking the main gate. No one was going inside the Rock for a few days. What a night. He'd had close calls, taken countless risks and broken many laws for a bundle of cash, but tonight was the worst. He gazed into the mouth of the tunnel, his heart sinking at the thought of what kind of mess the Pilkington twins had left for him to drag through the dark to his boat and slip to the fish in the Strait of Gibraltar. He shrugged. If it was too messy he'd ask for a few thousand more. They were good for it, and he could make life difficult for them if he chose.

He rattled the iron gate, the jangle of the chain

echoed down the chasm, and he turned away. A pink ribbon of light was brushing the grey sky to the east. The solo birdsong of a keen early riser drifted across from higher up the Rock. In less than an hour it would be light. The air was chilly and fresh.

Settling into the driver's seat, he started the patrol car, set the heaters on and the sound of a night-time smooth-jazz station wafted from the radio. Yawning, he pointed the car slowly down the single-track road and crawled through the dim dawn light. With a final twist of the wheel, he rounded onto the tarmac main road at the base of Gibraltar's monolith.

And that's when he saw it. Something in the road, up ahead. He crept slowly onwards, peering, squinting. It was a person, limping, staggering down the centre of the road. As the distance between them shortened, he stopped the car. A couple of hundred metres away, the figure stopped and fell to its knees. He narrowed his eyes and flicked the headlights to full beam. It was a girl. He edged forward. She was kneeling in the middle of the road, shielding her eyes from the glare.

It was the hair that gave her away. Even from

this distance he recognised the straggly Afro braids of the girl he'd seen on the gurney.

'Huyyyyyy,' he groaned in disbelief. Then his heart raced. This wasn't just a defeated, half-dead girl in the beam of his headlights; this was a world of potential consequences. Sweat beaded on his brow as he checked his rear-view mirror. The road was dark. The road was empty. He pulled at his shirt collar and a gold crucifix tugged free from beneath. He held the cross to his lips as he watched the girl drop her head, exhausted.

'Dios perdoname,' he whispered. 'No loose ends.' He pushed his foot hard on the accelerator and closed his eyes.

Twenty

Sunshine, money, pleasure, death: one or more of these was on the minds of the tourists, commuters and delivery drivers in the hot, patient queue to pass the customs border into Spain. Among the bored pedestrians lining up to pass the small brick building stood a couple holding hands. Ed's battered and rebuilt prosthetic was concealed beneath combat pants. Mary's bandaged foot was poking through open-toe sandals, and the dressings on her arms and face were getting glances. She wore a large floppy sunhat to avoid prying eyes and carried an ivory silk parasol, a delicate family heirloom unblemished by the fire that had killed their parents. It had been almost a week since that chaotic, exhilarating, frustrating night, their foiled attempt to finally prove Ed's genius. It would be weeks more before her face could see the sun again.

'I'm so sorry, petal,' Ed said, tenderly kissing her nose.

'*I'm* sorry! I should have been more … I don't know. Alert.'

'You were brilliant. Don't be silly.'

The line shuffled on as their private, hushed conversation continued in the shade of the parasol. 'Do you regret it, Edward? Do you regret what happened?'

'No! Not at all. It was a setback, Mary, that's all.'

'Really?'

'Of course. We know the chemistry, we have the money, we can start again. And there's no shortage of volunteers.'

She squeezed his hand and they arrived at the Customs window, where a familiar cracked-leather face curled into a ghoulish grin.

'Buenos dias, Hector,' smiled Ed.

The bulldog returned a grunt. 'How long will you be spending in España?'

'Oh just the day,' Mary cheerfully replied.

Ed handed over their passports. Below the frame

of the window, out of sight, Hector opened them, slid out the crisp, beige 200-euro notes tucked between their pages, and said, 'Wait please. I check details.'

Mary heard a tutting from behind her in the queue. 'Sorry,' she smiled to the woman, who visibly gasped at Mary's swollen, blistered face.

Hector slid a USB stick into his computer and with a couple of taps on his keyboard brought up the faces and passport details of Carly, Dane and Petra.

'It's a beautiful day to visit the mainland,' Mary said cheerfully to the embarrassed woman, who returned a curt nod before retreating behind her newspaper. Mary read the headline, 'Tourist found dead after night climb', and saw enough of the first paragraph to read that the body of Krishna Puram had been discovered at the foot of a steep drop at the Rock's edge. Drinkers at the Luna Rossa bar reported that the British data analyst had announced that he was going to climb the Rock after a substantial drinking session. Police confirmed the death as 'unexplained but not suspicious' and were not seeking anyone else with regard to the investigation. Death by misadventure, thought Mary.

While she was reading the woman's newspaper-partition, Hector, unseen by anyone but Ed, hit the 'Return' key on his keyboard three times. 'Uno, dos, tres …' he murmured, sending the faces of Carly, Dane and Petra sliding across his screen. He held Ed and Mary's passports on his scanner and added, 'cuatro, cinco' as their photos slid across the screen to join the others. 'Cinco personas.' He slid the two passports back across to Ed and said, with no hint of joy, 'Welcome to España.'

Epilogue

'Hey, Mom, look!' the child shouted. A young boy in a Seattle Mariners baseball shirt and ripped jeans was yanking on his mum's arm.

'I know, I know,' replied the boy's tired mother. 'A monkey.'

A slow straggle of tourists, like obedient ants, were winding up and down the Rock of Gibraltar, the late summer sun casting blooms in perfect light against the shadow of the grey peak. Among countless pairs of eyes, those of the seven-year-old saw something unique.

'But look!' he persisted, tugging on her arm.

The woman seemed unimpressed by the Rock

and keen to leave. 'Caleb, giddy-up,' she scolded. 'If we stop to look at every goddam ape on this place we'll never get to the stores, and Mom needs to buy aunt Suzie's cigarettes before we get back on the ship. Now c'mon!'

'But Mom, looook!' he whined. 'That monkey's got a phone!'

She stopped and followed his gaze. Sure enough, tucked within the thicket on the slope, an inquisitive ape was turning a grey smart-phone over in its hands. 'Well, I'll be ...' uttered the woman. The ape squeezed, shook and tested the device between its teeth. 'Hey, Kyle,' she said, 'maybe he's calling his friend the elephant, makin' a *trunk* call, geddit?'

The boy didn't respond.

She quietly added, 'You wouldn't get that. But you're grandma woulda loved that joke.'

The ape grew bored and tossed the phone, which spun through the air, landing a couple of paces from the boy's feet. Before his mother could protest he'd leapt into the grass, reached high into the weeds and retrieved it. He held it up, victorious. The woman's shoulders slumped. 'Caleb, honey, I –'

'WOAHHH,' he cried, examining his prize.

195

'This is *awesome!* D'you know how much these things cost?'

'Honey, it's trash.'

'Can I keep it, Mom? Pleeeease?'

She checked her watch and buckled instantly. 'Fine. But can we go?'

The boy gave a victory cheer and started closely inspecting the phone. 'It's not even cracked. But it's dead.'

'I don't want you to build your hopes up, sweetie. If that's what I think it is, people don't just throw away a thousand dollar phone. It's either lost or busted, and if it's lost, well –'

'Awwww, Mom!' He knew where this was going. 'Who'm I gonna hand it *in* to? This coulda been here *weeks!*'

'True, I guess. But, it'll be locked, is all.' He pondered this as they walked down the path. After a minute of silence between them, she offered some hope. 'How 'bout this: when we get back to the cruise ship we'll plug it into my charger, see what happens.'

Acknowledgments

A huge thank you to these wonderful people - horror fans Bethan, Edie and Ella Courtie for each reading early drafts and giving great notes. Pete Gardner for his forensic ability to uncover plot holes and loose ends. Jerry Tremain for leading us through the tunnels of the Rock and sharing his amazing knowledge. Russel McLean and Martin Ouvry for their editorial expertise. And finally, thanks to the lovely Gibraltarians for their friendship, hospitality and excitement at this project. Reader, I recommend a visit.

Stay out of the tunnels at night.

CONTACT THE AUTHOR
simeon@simantics.tv

FOLLOW THE AUTHOR
@simcourtie on Twitter